MOON CREEK ROAD

collected stories

Other Books by Elana Dykewomon

Riverfinger Women
Nothing Will Be As Sweet As The Taste
Beyond the Pale

MOON CREEK ROAD

collected stories

Elana Dykewomon

Spinsters Ink Books
Denver, Colorado
USA

First edition published April 2003
10-9-8-7-6-5-4-3-2-1

Spinsters Ink Books
P. O. Box 22005
Denver, CO 80222
USA

Cover Photography
Marilyn Lande

Interior Design:
Attention Media Group

ISBN 1-883523-62-1

Printed in Canada

MOON CREEK ROAD

collected stories

Elana Dykewomon

ACKNOWLEDGEMENTS

Thanks o thanks! to my generous lover, partner and proof-reader, Susan Levinkind; to my best critic and intimate, Dolphin Waletzky; to my favorite neighbor and jazz, Susan Jill Kahn; to my great reading tour companion Tryna Hope; to my excellent writing group collaborators Barbara Ruth and Teya Schaffer for invaluable critiques of these stories.

Much appreciation to my wonderful publisher at Spinsters Ink, Sharon Silvas, and my talented editor, Vicki P. McConnell.

Thanks to the following friends who have supported my life as a writer in various ways over the years: Andrea Krug, barbara findlay, Barbara Kuhne, Claire Kinberg, Caryatis Cardea, Chrystos, Cindy Chan, Dan Nachman, Diane Sabin, Dorothy Allison, Ellen Dean Cummins, Esther Rothblum, Eva Schocken, Evelyn Averbuck, Fan Warren, Frances Goldin, Gale Kissin, Gloria Anzaldúa, Glory Katz, Hadas Rivera-Weiss, Helen Mintz, Hilde Waletzky, Irena Klepfisz, Jan Hoffman, Jewelle Gomez, Jess Wells, Jo Keroes, Joan Drury, Joan Nestle, Judith Katz, Karen X. Tulchinsky, Karyn Sanders, Katherine Acey, Lee Lanning, Lilian Mohin, Linda Shear, Lisa Edwards, Louise Turcotte, Margo Rivera-Weiss, Marilyn Kallman, Michal Brody, Nancy Nordhoff, Pamela Gray, Rachel Nachman, Red She Bear, Rhea, Rose Weisberg, Ruth Gundle, Sally Koplin, Sheila Gilhooly, Susan Goldberg, Susan Stinson, Terry Hill, Toni Lester, Tova, Tracy Moore and Windflower.

Gratitude to: Cottages at Hedgebrook, The Helene Wurlitzer Foundation, Norcroft Writing Retreat for Women and Soapstone, a Writing Retreat for Women for their great gifts of time and solitude.

And thanks to the Astraea Foundation for a grant through the Loving Lesbians Fund in 1999.

CREDITS

"What Love Is," in *Best Lesbian Love Stories 2003,* Alyson Press, Los Angeles, 2003.

"Rebecca's Garden," in *Harrington Lesbian Fiction Quarterly,* Vol. 3, #2, Binghamton, NY, 2002.

"Antelope," in *Love Shook My Heart II,* Alyson Press, Los Angeles, 2002.

"Dinoflagellates," *Hot & Bothered 3,* Arsenal Pulp Press, Vancouver, 2001.

"Grace, B.C.," in *Augenblicke,* Krug & Schadenberg, Berlin, Germany, 1999.

"The Bottom," *Hot & Bothered 2,* Arsenal Pulp Press, Vancouver, B.C., 1999.

"Knaydle and the Librarian," in *Friday the Rabbi Wore Lace,* Cleis Press, San Francisco, 1998.

"Sliding" as "Prologue," in *Transfer 71,* San Francisco, Spring 1996.

"The Vilde Chaya and Civilization," in *Bridges,* Vol. 3, No. 1, Eugene, OR, Spring/Summer, 1992.

"My Grandmother's Plates," in *Speaking for Ourselves—Short Stories by Jewish Lesbians,* Crossing Press, Freedom, CA, 1990.

"Salt of the Earth," in *Naming the Waves,* Crossing Press, Freedom, CA, 1989.

"The Story I Never Write," in *Sinister Wisdom,* #36, Berkeley, CA, Winter 1988/89.

"Staking Claims," in *Common Lives/Lesbian Lives,* #17, Iowa City, IA, Fall 1985.

"The Mezuze Maker," in *Common Lives/Lesbian Lives* #8, Iowa City, IA, .1983.

"My Grandmother Play," staged by Luna Sea Productions, San Francisco, July, 2000.

Most of the stories previously published have been modified for this collection.

This book is dedicated
to the lesbian & women's press movement.

TABLE OF CONTENTS

PREFACE

The stories in this book were written between the early 1980s and 2002. Some of them have been published in journals and anthologies, but I never attempted to see them as a whole until I started putting this collection together.

The collection surprised me by becoming linked episodes about a group of friends and lovers; by its exploration of the way "mental illness" marks lives; by its juxtapositions of spirit world, death and sexual impulse; by its collage presentation of specific lesbian lives and social issues.

For me, the book is about taking the journey, about finding a way where everyone has told us no way exists. As a Jew outraged by the actions of the Israeli state, as an American appalled by the imperial arrogance of the country I reap the uneasy privileges of living in, as a lesbian—I exist in the vulnerable state of having no homeland, no sense that any place in the world "belongs" to me. Except the stories we make together.

What I hope, and keep hoping, is that lesbians of every kind will find room in the world for their own stories. And that eventually (sooner rather than later) borders will stop making sense because our stories will no longer hinge on the empty language of turf, possession and competition, but on the visions we bring to relationships. May our words remake the world.

—Elana Dykewomon

MOON CREEK ROAD

Two dykes in a blue pickup truck ramble along a back road. They stop at a river. One of them, Kasha, wades in and picks up a long flat stone.

The other, Phyllis, who is not as spry, stands on the low bank and says, "Who do you think you are, Moses?"

"Yup—but I'm going to write my own commandments."

The river is copper. It appears as if lit from underneath, and runs over beds of smooth granite or shale, scooped out in places, as if a woman had taken a giant melon baller and served up the river bed as fruit salad for the Gorgons' picnic. The river runs between shadows. Phyllis says they're cast by aspen, since it's too far west for birch.

"No, not aspen—alder," Kasha counters, even though she claims her memory is shot from smoking dope. Aspen, alder, birch—different sections of the country, almost in thirds. They studied the shaded guides delineating the territories of trees on nature trails when they came west three years before. In this part of the country, it's alders. Today they are at the base of the Oregon coastal hills, on Moon Creek Road.

You hardly ever see women riding around on the long coastal range stretches, logging roads and back tracks through the mountains. If you're lucky, have a good sense of direction and an understanding of maps, you can avoid getting dead-ended in a mud puddle beside a barbed wire fence. Mountain roads don't always go where the maps indicate. One time, coming back from

Eugene, they found what could best be described as a path, below the summit where the snow sticks through May. Rumbling over the dirt ruts, they came across wild darlingtonia lilies. Kasha and Phyllis had studied a trail guide about them, maybe a year before, in a native carnivorous flower preserve on Route 101, well-marked and roped-off. Phyllis had never seen them anywhere else—except on the side of that mountain pass, in a quick glance, while she was trying to control the truck. A carnivorous flower.

"Your face is a carnivorous flower," Phyllis says, although Kasha is the vegetarian.

"Don't talk dirty to me like that," Kasha kicks at the water, sending a wave toward Phyllis.

"Why not?"

"Because here I am, holding the holy tablet in the middle of the river."

"Bet I could make you drop it."

"Why would you want to?" Kasha looks soft and bewildered.

"Oh, you're no fun." Phyllis pitches a stone into the water. She takes her shoes off and cools her flat feet. The river's course is too jagged and narrow for swimming, though they could tangle naked in the shallows if they wanted to. No one ever comes down Moon Creek Road. Phyllis sits on a rock and regards Kasha, who has the dark curls and scraggly chin hair of an old testament prophet. We forget how young those prophets were—probably no older than thirty-five, the same as Kasha.

Righteousness, belief in reformation, certainly those are youthful propositions, propositions that still ache like a burn scar in Phyllis's lungs. Kasha's always making fun of her cynicism, her ennui. "You act like you're the older one, but you can't teach your grandmother to suck eggs," Kasha says whenever Phyllis starts lecturing about the way the world is. Phyllis grimaces and then hopes she hasn't been observed. Why shouldn't she make Kasha drop her tablet? If she doesn't, this rock will get thrown in the back of the truck and added to the mess of bird wings, eucalyptus buttons, transparent snake sheddings and crystals that litter the small house they rent, three miles from the sea.

Remote as their wood-heated home is, Phyllis is amazed at the way women keep showing up at their door. She came to Oregon because she was sore from fighting with lesbians on the East Coast. She met Kasha along the way; they paired up in a tent in Florida, where Kasha's dog bit a ranger who promptly kicked them out of the state park. Phyllis was determined to make it to the Oregon coast, a place she'd longed for since her first glimpse of it in college, and was glad that Kasha wanted to come along. Kasha was extravagantly generous in gesture, affection, money, loyalty, time—when Phyllis woke to the alarm clock for her job at the Bandon Historical Society, she'd find a plate of hot muffins and a pail of blueberries Kasha had snagged at dawn from the gone-to-seed U-Pick lot across the highway. At first, Phyllis was charmed.

"Your face is a carnivorous flower," Phyllis repeats, almost to herself, because she likes how it sounds.

But Kasha hears her. "You're the carnivore here. Why don't you try to eat me and see what happens?"

"I think not today. Not unless you drop the commandments."

"Was I commanding you?"

"You never think you do." Phyllis plinks another rock, which sinks ten feet from Kasha.

"What's that supposed to mean?"

"Nothing."

Phyllis believes she loves their coastal life, the years that no one would have predicted for urban Jews. When Kasha is in San

Francisco, bedding down acquaintances (with Phyllis's blessing), Phyllis looks out her country window and notices the sour cherry tree is dropping more fruit on the ground than even the birds can eat. She goes out to pick cherries in her old "Parthenogenesis" T-shirt, which becomes speckled with cherry stains across its expanse. Then she pits the cherries, rolls out whole-wheat dough, and makes a pie. An afternoon entirely spent making a sour cherry pie from scratch—she considers it a form of religious experience, an exercise in being present, in being satisfied with providing your own satisfaction.

After Phyllis moved back to the city, she sometimes dreamt that she was driving along a map of Oregon. First she was in a car, then on foot. The road became separated by doors, behind the doors, broken sections of road. Sections of road that echoed a version of lost paradise—rock cliffs drenched with moss, waterfalls, cascades of ferns, and an embankment on the other side leading down into cool, shaded, perfect streams. She dreamt of dirt roads and days when there was enough time to take the long way. Douglas fir climbed the slope across the river. In the dream, someone was with her for awhile. Then she was gone.

Dust moves up through the light, into the alder leaves. Moon Creek Road goes up the side of the mountain in abrupt switchbacks, once it crosses the field of alders and this little copper stream. The road hangs to a path along the mountain, then drops down hard, with a full view of the sensuous range of hills from the left. To the right are the logged-off slopes. You can almost imagine you see to the ocean but you can't, not quite. Kasha's stone tablet rattles in a box in the back of the pickup.

Phyllis wants time away from the houseguests. Kasha welcomes anyone who comes to the door or calls from Bandon—even Germans who are traveling around the U.S. in August after the Michigan Women's Music Festival, who often get Kasha's name from one of her old lovers. Despite being the daughter of a holo-caust survivor, Kasha welcomes the Germans in, even makes soup for them. Phyllis and Kasha share a childhood full of fairytales; all over the world people tell a story of gods, angels or spirits who come disguised as beggars.

A stranger at your door could represent some other power, the unseen one, checking up on your generous heart. Kasha and Phyllis hold in common an unstated belief that failed generosities count against you. But Phyllis lives with the certainty that the stink of a secret selfishness is on her breath and can't fathom why Kasha doesn't smell it. She begins to consider Kasha's love a will-ful, at best naive, state of misperception.

The evening before Phyllis's dog died, she drove Moon Creek Road alone, while she waited for Kasha to get back on the mid-night bus from Seattle. The golden retriever she'd had for eleven years lay in a cage at the vet's, unable to come out of seizure. In the late purpling light, a river otter crossed Phyllis's path. Further up the mountain on a steep, narrow curve, she knew something else was coming—a presence as big as a logging truck. She pumped the brakes, hugged the edge of the track, hoping to survive the collision. Then two elk ran by, on either side of her. Huge elk, running, turning their eyes to meet hers for a moment, telegraphing *kiss your dog goodbye.*

Kasha reaches for Phyllis, but Phyllis keeps her eyes on the road, her hands on the wheel. The road dips, bends, rises, curves, curves, crescents, makes a wider crescent, an arc, as it approaches the ridge. Just below the summit, she stops the car. The hill above her slopes back and spreads itself outward from a deep crease. Yellow and purple lupine edge the crease, and water slides through that long black line down to a boulder, around it, under the road, then over the side of the mountain. She feels as if she has come before the secret. This is the very nub of the world, the genesis rock, from which breath itself springs.

Kasha bounds out of the pickup and stands in the meadow, hands pressed together at chest level, as if she's praying. Turns out she is praying, bowing to the four directions. This vaguely annoys Phyllis, who does not like the language of altars or of reverence, although she is reverent, if she's alone on the road, with no one watching. She stays in the truck for awhile, then moves slowly to stand at the edge of the mountain, breathing consciously, feeling the coolness the moss gives off. Does the Earth have a belly button, an umbilical cord, did it drop out of the flaming bowels of creation, was it attached in a thousand places, here?

Kasha comes up to her. "What a view!"

"It is beautiful," Phyllis says, and smiles. Kasha puts her hands on Phyllis's shoulders, looks into her eyes, and kisses her, a wet kiss, with a tentative surge of tongue. Phyllis responds with her lips.

"We're the same size," Kasha says, which always makes Phyllis laugh since she's almost twice as wide. "Don't laugh. You know what I mean."

"I know what you mean," Phyllis says, as if that's an agreement. As many fat women do, she meditates frequently on the meaning of size—size of belly, size of intention, size of desire. She chooses to live in coastal Oregon because she fits into the landscape. This fit is a private thing, like squeezing into your favorite jeans when they're hot out of the dryer, before they give. Phyllis doubts that Kasha can understand this, and isn't willing to explain. In fact, she isn't willing to realize that they have not talked about it. She is content to let Kasha believe their journeys are in sync, a prickly sync, but close enough to make a home.

After awhile Phyllis starts the pickup and Kasha leaps in. Both of them are busy with looking at the creased meadow. The road crests several hundred feet up, then descends through logging trails, dozens of easy-to-get-lost-on tiny forks, places where last year's floods left the mud treacherous with piled tree trunks, difficult to pick through, but cleared enough for the heavy logging trucks.

It's a long time, half an hour at least, before the rutted track empties into a larger paved road beside a thick gush of river, thirty, forty feet wide. Pulloffs are marked with the logging company's logo, indicating they're on logging land. Then the company's little green houses appear—for the timber manager, the guy who runs the scales and bunks for men so they can be there at first light. For awhile, the cliff is sheer again on the right. Suddenly a little tin roof juts across the road—where the loggers have diverted a waterfall. Driving under it, they hear the fall detour on the corrugated tin above them. Phyllis stops to stick her arm out the window, into the curtain of water. Then she and Kasha get out of the car and let the water bouncing off the tin fall on their heads, as they dance. They've always admired a waterfall, wherever they found one. Women say waterfalls change your energy—something about negative ions.

Perhaps, Phyllis thinks, smiling at Kasha. She wonders whether the strangers back at their house have done any damage with the wood stove. Kasha takes her hand. Phyllis lets her, though she shies from the intimacy and cannot let Kasha know. Phyllis closes up, a carnivorous flower, determined not to eat the fly at her aperture.

Several miles later, the road bumps into the back yard of the lumber company itself. Full of men and vehicles and offices, buildings and stacks of downed trees. That's where the road ends and begins, according to the lumber company. Driving out of the yard, they pass a guard booth. The guard, occupied with an incoming truck, waves their pickup on without looking. Turning around, they can make out the sign—"Authorized vehicles only." A woman in a car, two dykes, could never get past the guard.

They'd have to know the other way. Up Moon Creek Road, where you hardly ever see women driving alone.

CANOEING

Phyllis came from immigrants who worked in cloth. Some of them prospered, some did not, but they all trekked out of the eastern cities to Lake George every summer, as they had since the 1920's. She had a childhood memory of a canoe, relatives rowing, old stories about storms coming up suddenly and acts of great bravery. When she was twenty-one, she stopped at the lake once to visit. Her Uncle Gabe was pleased to furnish a tour in his powerboat, since it afforded him the outdoor opportunity for a cigar. He used it to point to the island where her great grandmother and great aunt spent Augusts alone. "They would take a canoe and supplies," he said, flicking ash in the water," and tell everyone not to worry or bother them. They didn't have a lot of use for us. Tough old gals." Later, at dinner, when she was showing off to a younger cousin how she could touch her nose with her tongue, Gabe said, "Very nice. But what good is a double-jointed tongue?" She refused to tell.

At the end of the '70s, Kasha found Phyllis in Florida, living in a van. A funky van, with two single cots stacked above each other in the back, a propane refrigerator that never worked right, a serviceable stove, a tiny closet for a toilet designed to turn into a shower, a sink, a table that unhinged to stretch across the booth so it could become a kind of couch. *Arvee,* Phyllis called it, as if it might hold its own with the behemoths of summer highways. Once it had been a bakery truck. Everything in it was barely a little better than falling apart, but it could be plugged in and hooked up, a lesbian could live in it on the road, and Phyllis was.

She was holing up in her van and had made it to the north-east shore of Florida, where lesbians running guest cottages had agreed to let her plug into the main house if she promised self-sufficiency and paid $60 a month in rent. She hadn't been there a week when Kasha drove up with Louise. Phyllis knew them superficially from the town they were all fleeing. There had been a terrible clash of opinion, rumor, innuendo, political debate, adolescent personality, as the local women's movement splintered, or, as some suggested, was infiltrated by government agents. Centrifugal force flung the participants outward through the Americas. Some went to Cuba, Nicaragua, Quebec, Vancouver or Minneapolis, but most headed for San Francisco. Phyllis was damned if she was going to go to California with the New Age crowd, and headed her truck in what she thought to be the most unlikely direction—south.

It was a beautiful ride. The Blue Ridge Mountains swelled into curves, then split into hazy ribbons. "Panoramic," the signs said, panoramic vista, and the signs were right. Why fight the park service? Closet poets work for the government too. Along the route, lesbians were hospitable to Phyllis in D.C., Asheville and Georgia, but the best moments were camping with her dog. At sunset as she leaned on a chained-down picnic table, trying to sketch hanging moss with chalky pastels, deer showed up scavenging for leftovers but emanating grace. Phyllis was pleased with herself for making a clean escape, and still being capable of wonder and joy. Rocking the van's narrow bunk at night with her hands on her own flesh, she was reluctant to remember either the community or the lover she'd left. Left her. She'd left. Reluctant to go anywhere that would remind her of them. Counting her luck: Arvee and Grindle, the golden retriever; the money she'd saved at her first real job, being a glorified secretary and bouncer for a social service agency that administered Section 8 housing assistance to the handful of applicants who could negotiate its bureaucratic maze.

On the road south, the air tasted like cinnamon—a familiar excitement, the freedom to use as much spice as you liked. No more desperate women on the phone, either at her job or at home. Arriving in St. Augustine, she got the tour of the Florida cottages, plugged Arvee into a socket with her red heavy-duty extension cord, and went for a walk on the beach. Calm, happy, no mail, no messages. She turned back to make herself dinner. "Grindle," she called.

Someone said, "I know a dog named Grindle."

Phyllis looked up. Two short, Jewish women in their thirties stared back.

"And I know you!" The one who was Kasha grinned.

Phyllis was amazed to see Kasha and Louise, whom she had known tangentially up north, attending the same concerts and conferences. Everyone started to hug, but pulled back, not remembering if they were on different sides of an argument, if their ex-lovers had hated each other. Something about Kasha's ex's sister who had allegedly scratched the finish on Phyllis's ex's ex-roommate's used Saab. Something that happened on a grand jury committee. Stiff hugs all around. Kasha and Louise were not lovers—only traveling together, out west, to San Francisco they thought, if a little circuitously, to change their lives.

Phyllis went back to her van, turned on her tiny black and white TV, and decided the best course was to ignore them.

Of course Kasha and Louise stayed. After all, it was warm, the beach was empty and clean. The next afternoon, Phyllis was walking down the shore and saw Kasha, dressed entirely in white, curls in disarray around her cheeks, sitting at the edge of sand by the beach plums. Phyllis walked a ways past her, and then faced the ocean. Faced the ocean, the salt dissolving into green, the green flickering with salt and refraction, piling clear up in peaks until the light winced through it on both sides, and it came all over itself, translucent. She took a deep breath and turned her thick body around to face the woman waiting for her.

Kasha was casting the I-Ching. Phyllis never had. She knew something about the Tarot, but stayed suspicious of everyone's motives for dabbling in mystic arts from cultures about which they knew diddly. Not only cultural appropriation, but the invasion of symbols into the mind. Symbols change the course of minds, and who knows what spirit lurks behind the symbol, how male or malevolent it may have been, what ancient code a symbol might use to take you in. Once a woman had turned over the three of swords and said to Phyllis, "This means three disasters will happen, three knives through your heart." Could the woman really foretell the griefs that came to pass, or had Phyllis manufactured them in order to fulfill the prophecy?

Despite her doubts, Phyllis sat beside Kasha, and learned how to cast the I-Ching. Her reading was along the lines of: *Cross the great water. She takes her meals with strangers. Good fortune on the path.*

Then Kasha reached in her pocket and pulled out a collection of glass beads and stones. This in particular impressed Phyllis, whose pockets bulged with at least her Swiss army knife, a piece of amethyst her ex-lover had given her, a piece of quartz she liked, a tiny rubber dinosaur, several shells, three pens and all her keys.

"Take anything," Kasha said.

"Really? You mean it?" Phyllis, if she'd ever been moved to make such an offer, would not likely have meant it, not fully.

"Anything. Go ahead."

Phyllis chose two beads, one black and white with a little donkey painted on it, and one glass, striped green and purple.

Kasha found the memory of that first night together in Arvee particularly fragrant, sweet as an antique purple rose. They stayed up all night talking, watching TV, and Phyllis inked "I like to keep my jubilee in easy reach," on the window sill, a line from the show they were watching.

"And then our thighs brushed as we stood up and passed each other in the van—" Kasha always said, with electric static emphasis on the word "brushed."

But Phyllis remembered something else. How she, Kasha and Louise were sitting in a diner off the interstate, drinking coffee, three days later. Louise and Kasha had to move on. Would Phyllis join them? Coffee was a nickel a cup. Phyllis was looking at the stretch marks steam makes across the face of coffee, sorting old sorrow and new lust. She shredded her napkin, making piles out of the debris to represent her several definitions of freedom.

Kasha was punching the jukebox, settling on Bonnie Tyler who sang, "It's a heartache, nothing but a heartache." One, twice, six times, Kasha kept playing it. "Alright, I'll come along with you for awhile—but for god's sake, don't play that song again," Phyllis said. Adventure seemed likely as a trio, caravanning through the South, but it meant thinking of Kasha as other than a one night stand. In the diner, she abandoned her solitary recovery and moved on to camp in a state park thirty miles down the road.

When Louise went shopping in Daytona, Kasha and Phyllis sweated, naked, gliding all over each other in the hot October afternoon, glad for the room to spread out in a two person tent with the sleeping bags unzipped across the floor, after bruising their elbows in the confines of Arvee. Kasha had a long sexual hunger, and Phyllis was dazed by her ability to bring pleasure, by Kasha's ability to take. The noise of the several worlds she inhabited, past and present, dropped away as she listened for the sharp intake of Kasha's breath before she came. So she didn't hear the footsteps.

But Kasha's mutt, Zelda, did. No dogs are allowed in Florida state parks. Zelda broke through the tent's netting and leaped at the approaching ranger, tearing his pants and drawing blood.

When Louise came back from shopping, she found Phyllis, Kasha and the dogs waiting by the park's entrance gate. "I can't leave you alone for a minute," she complained, with an edge of admiration in her voice. They decided to drive on to the Everglades that night, since Federal land allowed dogs.

The campground at the Everglades was next to deserted when they arrived. The woman at the ranger booth admitted she'd hoped to be posted to California, where she came from. And cautioned them that it was mosquito season.

Mosquitoes the size of ping pong balls rammed themselves against every possible entrance, window, screen. Louise couldn't stay in the tent—the mosquitoes were too thick. And snakes, there might be snakes. They'd seen some.

So Louise came into the van and curled up on the little couch made for kids that kept falling down. The dogs snored in the aisle, under the driver's seat. Phyllis and Kasha behaved for Louise's sake and slept separately in the bunks, not squished almost on top of each other, defying the constraints of mechanical possibility. They all swatted and cursed bugs through the night, leaving trails of blood on the simulated-wood paneling.

Anyone with sense would have left the Everglades the next day and gone into Miami to find a good deli. These three decided to rent a canoe.

These three were women in their late twenties who came from families that had not embraced the outdoors as a way of life—summers and great grandmothers at the lake notwithstanding. All of them were short and of medium strength. Of them,

Kasha was the only one who had any experience canoeing, and that on lakes at Yiddish camp in the summer. Phyllis recalled vaguely that canoeing on the Everglades was something her mother would have warned her not to do, if it had crossed her mother's mind that she might ever possibly be so inclined. But Louise assured Phyllis that since she had survived canoeing with Kasha in the Okefenokee Swamp, the Everglades would be a snap.

And it seemed easy. The rented canoe glided slick through the narrow channel. Giant spiders made sparkling four-foot webs among ferns, birds aired out their wings in the sun, everything was big and bright. Even their mosquito repellent seemed to work.

Kasha took off her shirt and smeared herself with Everglade mud when they stopped to pee and eat lunch on a small, damp beach. Phyllis wasn't sure, but she thought she ought to find Kasha covered with swamp dirt charming in a back-to-Mother-Earth way. After eating, they scooted through the channel without much effort, and came into a large opening of the water system where many other channels appeared to branch in thirty-five directions. As they tried to decide which way to go and how to proceed without getting lost, sudden rain enveloped them.

"We have to go back." Phyllis tried to hold annoyance out of her tone.

Kasha slipped her shirt on, which became streaked with mud. She was sitting in the middle of the canoe. Louise was in front, Phyllis in back, and the two of them were paddling with all their strength, yet going nowhere. "Zig zag," Kasha said.

"Easy for you to say," Louise grumbled, huffing as she churned the water.

From bank to bank they zigged, zagged, painfully slow.

"You said you knew how to canoe," Phyllis said. "Didn't you think to check the current against which we were going to row back?"

"I never canoed in the Everglades before—actually, never on a river—only lakes. But it's an adventure, isn't it?"

"Adventure, adshmenture," Louise muttered, heaving.

The canoe began filling with rain. They had books and cameras with them, loose in the bottom, which they covered as best they could by sticking them underneath the seats.

Motor boats going back to the docks passed them. Zip, went the motorboats while Phyllis and Louise made another slow zag. "Want a tow?" someone hollered, but Kasha shouted that they were fine. The boat went on. Phyllis turned back to look at Louise, who held up a palm beginning to blister, which Phyllis matched with her own. "Okay, the next one," Louise said.

A large boat flying a confederate flag slowed as they waved it down. A burly, affluent man grunted at them and threw them a line that they tied to their bow. The man jerked both boats as he restarted his engine, and Phyllis had a moment of panic, holding her pocket knife, wondering how fast she could cut the rope. Never put yourself in a position to depend on men or have to be nice, that was her philosophy, but what good was a philosophy like that in the Everglades? It turned out the guy towing them was only sloppy—mostly he kept a steady slow speed, turning around once to take stock of them, and then, not interested in what he saw, proceeding.

A small speedboat cruised by, turned around, cruised back and deliberately cast a wave over the canoe. The guys in the speedboat sneered, saluted with their beer cans and gunned forward. Swamped, the women's gear started floating out from under the seats. Then the canoe sighed into the murky water. Louise was dogpaddling, holding her camera up, shouting to the man who was towing them, "Hey, hey! The canoe is sinking!"

Phyllis was trying to save the cushions; Kasha grabbed the paddles and her copy of Truman Capote. They were all yelling, screaming, until finally the pilot turned around and laughed, but stopped the boat.

"Is this dangerous?" Louise asked, as she treaded water, trying to gather everything that was floating.

The man kept laughing. "Could be," he said.

Louise hauled herself into the larger boat first, then Kasha. Phyllis had a lot of trouble, until Louise and Kasha each took an arm and pulled her up. Only the tip of the canoe showed by now, at the end of the rope. The man, still chuckling, started up again slowly. Ten seconds later he punched Kasha in the arm.

"What?" She asked, pulling away.

He pointed. An alligator, two alligators, crossed the boat's path. They nosed the canoe. "Dangerous," he said.

Kasha, Louise and Phyllis left the Everglades the next morning and kept their caravan going, Arvee following Louise's brown Plymouth station wagon around the curve of the Gulf of Mexico. They ate oysters all the way to New Orleans, judging the oyster bar in Tallahassee (six stools at a counter serving only oysters and Orange Crush soda) the best. After New Orleans, they parted company—Louise had grown weary of listening to Kasha and Phyllis Motel Six's walls since they left Florida. She had a friend in Austin she could hang out with. Kasha and Phyllis followed a meandering arc to the West Coast, visiting their mothers and the abandoned cliff dwellings of the Anasazi along the way.

Phyllis meant it—she would not live in California. She wanted nothing to do with hippies or beautiful pretenders to art or revolution, who, she believed, comprised the majority of the white population under forty. She had promised herself someday she'd live on the coast of Oregon, and she kept her promises.

"You know, the last time I really wanted something, it was to be the first woman to play baseball in the major leagues," Kasha said. "I'm not attached to living in California. If you want to live in Oregon, why not? But I think I'll hang out in San Francisco for awhile until you check it out. If you find someplace you like, I'll come join you."

San Francisco was stocked with women they knew who had been flung out of the collapse of their East Coast social system in a lesbian recreation of the big bang theory. Ex-lovers who'd made a more direct cross-country trip had hauled Kasha's belongings with them. She promised to retrieve them from storage to furnish whatever apartment Phyllis might find in Oregon.

Phyllis had everything she owned with her in Arvee. She made her way up the coast, and within a week moved out of the campground at Bastendorf Beach in Charleston and into an apartment with a view of the Coos Bay channel, a hundred miles from the California border. Kasha got friends to drive up with her, pulling her belongings behind a banged-up green Chevy Nova she'd bought in The City, and they settled into homemaking—Kasha and Phyllis, who had been lovers for eight months. They applied for food stamps, and Phyllis looked for work. As far as they knew, they were the only lesbians, the only Jews, for hundreds of miles.

It was only a couple weeks before the isolation of the Oregon coast pushed them to drive over to Eugene. They found the address for the women's bookstore there in the *Lesbian Connection* newsletter. As it turned out, the lesbian running the store was having a barbecue that pleasant, grassy Saturday afternoon in June. She'd heard of Phyllis and Kasha—bookstore managers get coast-to-coast gossip—and women they knew were going to be there, would they show up if she invited them?

Of course. Phyllis had some notoriety among political dykes, which made her shy now, not knowing from which direction the conversation might ambush her, what opinions she'd be expected to agree with or oppose. Kasha had her own sexual fame; several of her ex-lovers had slept with women invited to the barbecue, who also knew good friends of Phyllis's.

Clara, who had an ex-lover in common with Kasha, introduced them to Tamuz.

"We know each other," Phyllis said.

"It's great to see you again." Tamuz had once been Nancy, sitting in Phyllis's living room back East, trying to decide whether or not she was really in love with another woman in the food coop where she worked, and whether or not that made her a lesbian. Phyllis waited. "We're having a Fourth of July picnic for separatists out on Crow's farm, will you come?" Clearly Tamuz had made her decision.

At the Fourth of July picnic, Tamuz proposed that the group take a canoe trip up the Willamette River. Tamuz had just graduated from a canoeing course and was enthusiastic about paddling with a bunch of dykes. Since no one had argued about meat versus tofu franks, or much of anything else, twelve of them decided they might manage an adventure together. They'd go one way down the river, and have cars in place at the other end.

Phyllis told the story about the alligators in the Everglades, but it didn't deter anyone.

"We don't have alligators in Oregon," Tamuz assured them. Phyllis could have sworn she meant, *we're too mellow for alligators.* But since Tamuz seemed so organized, Oregon so full of enlightened outdoorsy types, and they wouldn't have to row back against the current, Phyllis agreed, much to Kasha's delight.

On the appointed day, they met at an inlet. Eleven dykes showed up, and Tamuz brought four rented canoes. Phyllis was momentarily reassured watching Tamuz organize the assemblage, making everyone tie their belongings into plastic bags hooked onto the canoe seats with bungee cords, in case of capsizing.

"Capsizing?" A young woman in a flannel shirt with the sleeves cut off asked nervously.

"It's likely some of us will capsize at least once. Does everyone know how to swim?"

Phyllis, who considered herself a strong swimmer, scuffed at the dirt with her sneakers. Everyone said they could swim except the nervous one.

"Well, if you don't know how, you definitely should wear your life jacket. All of you should wear them, of course." Tamuz pointed to the stack in each canoe. "How many of you have been canoeing before?"

As it turned out, Kasha was the only other dyke with any canoeing skills—and since their last adventure, she could even claim to have navigated a river.

"I'll take three in my canoe, because clearly I have the most experience," Tamuz decided. Phyllis got in a canoe with Kasha and a tall, competent-looking dyke, Amanda. Kasha had picked her as the most likely dope-smoking dyke in the crowd, and she was right.

Tamuz gave a lesson on launching, using the paddles to steer and righting a capsized canoe. Phyllis was not impressed by anyone's learning curve, including her own. She hoped Kasha would decide not to smoke, but she wasn't about to appear controlling.

Tamuz looked out over the river. "You know, the last time I was here, it was much higher."

The woman in cut-off flannel, strapping on her life jacket, sighed in relief.

"It does go slower," Tamuz said, almost to herself, as if meditating on the nature of rivers. Then she turned to the group, settled three to a canoe and eager to start, "but low water also exposes a lot more rocks and tree stumps. Be careful to watch out for them."

Except for the one woman who couldn't swim, everyone used their life jackets as seat cushions. Phyllis might have worn hers, but it wouldn't have tied around her, and that was too much embarrassment in front of Amanda, the skinny stranger who was now exchanging tokes from a thick joint with Phyllis's girlfriend.

They watched Tamuz in the lead canoe pull out into the current, scrape against a tree trunk and immediately capsize.

"Just showing you what not to do!" she laughed. The water was only thigh deep—the women shook themselves off and climbed back in.

"If that's capsizing, it doesn't look so scary," Kasha said, turning to smile at Phyllis and Amanda. Kasha was in front, paddling happily, Amanda in back, keeping up with an easy, loping stroke. Phyllis, in the middle, had a moment of well-being, taking in eleven dykes on the river on a sunny day, the great Amazon revolution come to fruition.

The canoe ahead of them negotiated a small but quick bit of white water. "Oh, rapids, what a trip," Kasha giggled, lifting her paddle up as they entered a series of waves.

"Put your paddle in the water!" Phyllis shouted.

"Oh, yeah," Kasha said. She dug into the foam, throwing it behind her by the shovelful.

"Hey! You're dumping the river into the canoe—take it easy."

"Easy?"

"Try to stay in rhythm with me," Amanda yelled forward, "don't push so hard."

"Oh…" Kasha concentrated, apparently trying to feel Amanda's oars through the hull of the boat, remembering all the platitudes about going with nature, not against her. Suddenly they were on the other side, and the river was in a smooth lull, pushing them along. Kasha raised her paddle again, and Amanda steered languidly from the back.

"Well, we got through that." Amanda sounded eager for the next trial.

"You did good, once you remembered to paddle," Phyllis said, putting her hand on Kasha's shoulder.

"Thanks. Want a turn?"

"You think we can trade places without drowning?"

Kasha looked down at the clear bottom. "I don't think we can drown in three feet of water."

"No, probably not." Amanda laughed, holding the canoe steady with her oar.

Carefully, slowly, squatting low into their centers of gravity, they switched seats. The boat tipped, but not dramatically, and Phyllis found herself staring out at small waves that shivered toward her. They were still second behind Tamuz, and up ahead the river seemed to take a sharp right turn. Phyllis shaded her eyes with her hand and squinted to see better.

"You okay up there?" Kasha asked, relighting her joint, offering it to Amanda, who now declined.

"Yeah, I guess."

"Relax and lean into it. You'll be fine."

Someone was shouting from the lead canoe. They all looked ahead. The river made a ninety degree turn in front of them. At the nub of the bend, like some bony broken elbow, a huge granite boulder jutted out, creating what appeared to be a whirlpool around it. The women in Tamuz's canoe were paddling hard, with Tamuz shouting directions at them. Phyllis strained to make out what she was saying, but the wind and slap of water made it impossible to hear more than grunts. Tamuz's canoe cleared the bend.

"Oh shit." Phyllis sucked her lips together. Lesbians in the canoe in front of her, lesbians in the canoe in back of them, and Amanda were all yelling instructions. Hold the paddle up, down, on the right, on the left. Kasha was intoning, "That's okay, honey, that's okay, you're doing fine."

The water sucked them toward the boulder at the speed of sound. Phyllis's forearm muscles burned with effort, but she couldn't figure out how to direct the canoe bow straight, to jump ahead of the force grabbing them.

"Oh no!" one of the other women yelled—she thought it was Amanda. They were colliding with the rock sideways. Phyllis pulled her oar up a second before it would have snapped in two. The canoe skidded, popped against the rock and then rolled over.

Underwater, Phyllis watched as her glasses plunged toward the stream bed. Following them with her eyes, she headed down to grab them and then realized she was beneath a large shadow. She looked up to see that the canoe was on top of her, upside down, with the bags of their gear dangling on the bungees, about to knock into her. Her lungs shriveled into hard coals, stabbing her chest. Fuck the glasses. She changed directions underwater, struggling up. Her shoulder grazed the side of the boat, but she broke the surface and shook her head—she could make out the life jackets and paddles that had been thrown into a brackish pool behind the rock. The canoe was being held against the boulder by the current. She tried to turn around and see what happened to Amanda and Kasha, but roiling water obscured her diminished vision, and she only heard shouts and screams.

Phyllis gasped, then kicked forward to grab a floating paddle and life preserver. Feeling under the boat, she found a rope she could hold onto. At that moment, some change in pattern spit the canoe out into a fast surge that ran along the far shore of the river, against a canyon wall. Beyond reason now, she simply held on, along for the ride. Her legs started hitting rocks and submerged branches. *I could snap like a twig, like an oar.* She pulled her knees up.

She jetted past one of the other canoes. Squinting, she could barely make out that it was full of women, but she recognized Kasha's voice yelling, "Are you okay?"

"I'm fine!" she yelled back, although she already imagined herself washed up in an inaccessible tangle of downstream debris, body crushed and broken. The current hurried her past the lead canoe, which was being baled out. "Try to beach it!" someone yelled. There were only boulders on the banks on her side of the stream, and she couldn't maneuver out of the current.

Up ahead, a small sandy beach appeared through a rocky entrance. Adrenaline rush and force of will got Phyllis to shift the canoe to the left so that the current bonked it against a rock, impeding progress long enough for her to get a foothold on the slippery river bed. Phyllis threw the life jackets and oars up on shore, pulled the canoe in between rocks where it seemed moored, and sat exhausted, surveying the river. Canoeists waved as they went by, all of them wearing their life jackets. Gradually she felt a throb in her calf, and put her hand to it, which came up smeared with blood. She twisted her leg to survey the damage—superficial enough, she decided, feeling along her limbs, and poking at the bruise on her shoulder.

From down river, she heard the dykes shouting before she saw them—one of the other canoes had overtaken Tamuz's, and Kasha was in it, gesturing frantically at her.

"I'm OK," Phyllis yelled. "Are you? Is Amanda?"

"We were thrown onto the shallow side—we're fine," Kasha yelled, splashing out of the canoe to the beach, leaping over the rocks to hug Phyllis.

The other canoeists followed, the eleven of them scrambling over each other onto the tiny beach for reunion. "Is this the way separatists have to do everything?" someone asked.

"For sure," Tamuz answered, which made most of them laugh.

Phyllis's canoe was dented appreciably, but still water-worthy. She was declared heroic for saving the canoe and the paddles. She complained about losing her glasses. Why hadn't Tamuz suggested they tie their glasses on? "I will next time," Tamuz said.

"Next time," Phyllis repeated, her eyes going wide, but she didn't think Tamuz heard her.

The dykes dried themselves and regrouped. They ate lunch—whatever hadn't gotten too banged up or wet in the bottom of the canoes—muttering, trying to make the best of it. Tamuz attempted to placate them. "It's real easy going from here, I promise."

They had no choice. Small boys had spotted them and were throwing rocks from the cliff above and woods behind them. The only way to get to their friends waiting at the cars was over water. Everyone got back in the aluminum and fiberglass crafts, this time wearing their safety jackets, except for Phyllis, whose jacket still didn't fit. Besides, she was convinced she wouldn't come that close to dying twice in one day.

Tamuz was right. The river broadened, and the dangers were easily avoided. Someone started singing. Kasha's dope was too wet to make another joint, which relieved Phyllis. She joked with Amanda about the lesbian flotilla, the experience they were getting for fighting a war, and even let herself burn a little in the sun.

Amanda's lover had a big blue truck waiting at the end point. Amanda, Kasha and Phyllis all squeezed in. The canoes were in the truck bed and on top; the four of them were charged with making the best deal they could about the dent.

Sixteen lesbians reconvened at a Eugene pizza parlor, the river veterans with their lovers and housemates. They all split what the rental place charged for the ding in the canoe. Phyllis declined an offer for a collection to replace her glasses.

While the others ate, Phyllis's gaze moved beyond them, to those glasses spiraling toward the bottom of the river. For her, the canoe was still on the surface, at least ten feet above. It was silent in the center of the whirlpool, pressure ramming her chest from both sides. For years, she made the decision to go up again, where the women gathered together, and the canoe shadowed the current's texture.

THE MEZUZE MAKER[1]

I'm driving on home from Eugene with the dogs, I must be on one of the world's better river roads, the afternoon is water color hazy, and the canyon walls are dripping with green. I look up over the hill, and I can swear I see—a mushroom cloud. I think, *it could happen now.*

My stomach is all balled up. I say, *stop thinking like that; if you keep thinking like that, it might happen. If all the powerful and frightened women like you imagine it around the next bend, taking the turn fast and hard, the world's in trouble, sweetheart. It's up to you to protect it. With your fiercest imagination and will.*

On the other hand, I've been anxious and depressed, not sleeping well, maybe my fear is about something else. *Tired, I'm just tired,* I think to myself, and stop in Florence to eat a hot dog at the carnival they've set up overnight for the rhododendron festival, careful to leave water and the windows rolled down for Grindle and Fawn. Under the arcade tent, there's a guy hogging the one video machine I want—Ms. Pacman, my favorite. I'm jealous.

A barker entices me to shoot corks at little plastic fuzzy squirrels, two shots for fifty cents. The carnival grounds are kinda empty, it's the middle of a weekday afternoon. The woman in this booth says the squirrel shoot is one of her favorite things to do at the carnival. I miss my first two shots, and she gives me another shot on the house, pushing the little cork in the barrel. I knock the squirrel down on my third shot—something about the sights, I realize, are a little off.

Suspicious of everybody, ain't you, Phyllis? Yeah, well, I had a roommate once, in college, who'd run away one year to travel around as a carny. She told me about it. Phoebe and I lived on Bradley St. in some suburb of L.A. with this boy who had convinced himself he was a satanist. That was all right, he kept to himself, and he wasn't exactly dangerous. He was a real runty, smelly kind of white boy, and I figured he called up the powers on account of being so generally overlooked. Everyone wants a little power, that makes sense; men of course want it the way men want it, which doesn't make sense, but that's not important here. I keep trying to convince myself.

Anyway, I got used to being suspicious. When I was living with Phoebe and the satanist, I used to feel spirits in the house that the fool was messing around with, even when he wasn't there. So I learned to protect myself from them. Spirits are easy compared to bombs. You can tell a spirit to go away and if you put your heart into it, the spirit tends to respect you. Spirits, you know, they look for a way in. You've got a choice to give them one or not.

Phoebe had told me about the carnies and I remembered, aiming at those little plastic squirrels, who were celebrating the rhododendron festival in Florence the same as me. On my third try, I looked over the sights instead of through them, and that did the trick. For my prize, I got a little green plastic lei.

When I walked back over to the video arcade, the boy who was playing Ms. Pacman had left, and I threw my pocketful of change into the machine. What is violence? Is this violence? About a half hour later a guy comes up, smoking a cigarette, and leans against the machine in back of me. He does this male stuff, trying to push me out. I don't want to antagonize him. Sometimes it's a lot easier to deal with spirits when you want to hold onto your own space. I finish the game badly with him watching over my shoulder and leave without looking at him, but I can hear his quarter fall in the slot.

I decide it's time to do something different. I drive around Florence looking for the road to the ocean. Finally we get on Rhododendron Drive, the dogs get excited. Ten side streets and three dead ends later, we come to a pull over and the sweetest little slice of beach.

It's one of those gorgeous places—you climb down a sea wall, go over a little stream, and you're at the bottom of a huge dune. The Siuslaw River is at your feet, about a half mile from where it turns and runs into the Pacific, so it's kinda salty, I tasted it. You can see where the river shimmies into the open ocean way off to the right. The opposite bank is a fragile string of sand. Where I'm standing, you can't see the ocean, but you can feel it.

The dogs and I start walking down the beach. There's nobody but us and a million sea gulls, circling above. Some come down so low I swear I could reach out my hand and tickle their gray bellies. Maybe it's a nesting ground. The dogs are real happy—they've been in the car a long time. Grindle, my shaggy old retriever, goes in the water swimming, cooling off. Kasha's mutt Fawn, who looks like a cross between a coyote and a husky, tries chasing the gulls, which tease her.

I think, *damn this is beautiful—I want to remember this.* But inside I'm tight still. Maybe if one of the women I love was with me, we'd walk around this bend, where we couldn't be seen from the road, and lie in the warm sand, quiet and naked together. It's funny, I don't have an image of making love, but of looking at her arm in the sunlight—you know the way flesh is, that it carries thousands of little sparkles in the sunlight. Maybe it's the reflection of the light going through the hairs or something. *Maybe it's only Jewish skin,* I think, remembering the specific skin of Jewish women that I've loved in that particular way—where the little green and gold and red lights danced across the surface, and when I put my hand on her she was warm and smooth. But I'm alone, and I'm glad to be alone. I feel like too much of a wreck to be around anyone. *Tired,* I say to myself, *you're just tired.*

All of a sudden a siren goes off, in town somewhere, in long repeated blasts. It's around ten to four, so the siren makes no sense to me. A quiver starts in my scalp, prickles my back and runs down my calves. *Maybe this is the end. Here I am, on this beautiful beach, all alone at the end of the world, with the dogs.*

I try to get to a warmth inside me, to face the end with, but I can't. I'm scared. So I plant myself instead looking at the waves the wind makes across the width of the river, spread my feet, and start to pray.

I figure, I gotta do something, something for myself, if I'm going to be alone here and the world is coming to an end. Something to get all the little shot plastic squirrels and games of Ms. Pacman out of my mind. Dear Abby says that among the Jews, as long as you can say a brucha or do a mitsve,[2] you're still alive. So I figure I'll do a little mitsve for myself, and pray. To see if it gets their power off of me. When I pray, I thank. So I start thanking. And that helps.

I say out loud (there's no one around, and besides the world is ending, I can talk to myself if I want), "Thank you, goddess,[3] for the life I had." Then I think, *I'm still living.* So I say, "Thank you, for the life I have." Then I think, *maybe I'll go on living. Maybe if I concentrate, and even if the planet is dying, if I believe in my life and the life of the women I love, and all the women who are living and loving their lives and each other, trying to, anyway, maybe we'll be able to get somewhere else, keep going on, together.* So I say, "Thank you, goddess, for the life I will have."

I look at the bright sunlight refracting through the wave, which is about three inches high. I raise my head and look around at all the shapes of this place, their unwitting conspiracy to delight. The siren is still going. I say, "Thank you, goddess, for giving me this. For giving this. For the beauty of the world, for the luck I've had to see so much of it. For the luck of being able to love, for the women who've loved me. Thank you for love." I know it's pretty corny, but suppose it is the end—I have a right to say what I want.

I turn around. The sand is blowing gently against the layers of the dune behind me, and driftwood is piled in long narrow bands at its base. I think of making another mezuze.

Alone in the dark of a new moon last week I was frightened, with this same kind of nuclear fear, and Kasha woke to sit with me for awhile. I said, "What power do we have that can stop it, stop them from blowing the world up?" She didn't answer. My eyes got wet, but I didn't cry.

We had made a mezuze out of driftwood the week before for our friend Judy down in Oakland. Kasha painted a tree of life on it, and it was perfect, with the little prayer I wrote rolled up inside, in one of the corridors the sea makes in driftwood. The prayer goes: "The elements we respect protect us, Earth, air, fire, water and flesh, the lesbian element; heart, which is breath in us, clear eyes, open hands, magic, dreams and love." I wrote it in a circle, moving inwards. We painted chai[4] on the front.

I decided to start making mezuzes after going to the Danzig Exhibit, which featured Jewish ceremonial objects and photographs that the Danzig Jews sold to raise money so that everyone, no matter how poor, could get out of Danzig in 1939. They were sold on the condition that if a Jewish community was re-established in Danzig,[5] the objects would be returned.

I had been thinking about mezuzes, on and off, and in one of the cases at the exhibit, a beautiful wooden one lay on a purple cloth—I'd never seen a wooden mezuze—carved out of cherry. In the middle of the museum I thought, *I can make these.* So I went home and read in the bible all about what mezuzes were and what they were for. Then I changed everything.

Except that the ones we make still look like mezuzes, and they praise the spirit, and they are on the doorpost to both protect us and remind us of who we are, as we come and go from our homes. When we made the first one, and my lover and I hung it up on the doorpost, I felt glad, proud, and safe, in an unexpected way.

So when the night scared me, I said to Kasha, "We could make hundreds of mezuzes—we could hang them in the trees." It sounded crazy and desperate to me, but I didn't care. "We could make hundreds of them out of driftwood and give them to everyone, all our friends, and then the bombs couldn't fall. Because we would all be protected." She put her hand up against my cheek. I had an image of myself driven by my fear, hanging mezuzes on all the trees in the forest.

But I didn't find any good pieces of driftwood for mezuzes on the Florence beach. They have to be exactly right. They have to fit in your hand in a certain way. They have to fit for the woman you have in mind. The day I found the wood for Judy's, I understood that rummaging in the piles of driftwood, concentrating, gets a kind of spiritual feel to it. A very spiritual feel.

I thought about how my aunts said my grandmother was a pious woman. That tough old broad who lived on 86th St. in New York. She went to shul every Saturday, liked to watch the soap operas, and shock us, her grandchildren, by saying "shit" at the table.

You are losing it girl, I say to myself, taking a deep breath. I look up the beach. Another car has pulled off next to mine. Some tourists start poking around at the water and sand. The siren has stopped. *Try to stop thinking that the safety of the world is up to you, and find a way to enjoy this. Take a little pleasure. In the sunlight, in the day.*

I pat the dogs and tell them how good they are. I run with them a couple of steps in the soft sand. Then I walk back down the beach, climb up the sea wall, and head for home.

[1] A mezuze is a Jewish ritual object which is traditionally nailed on the doorposts of Jewish homes, for protection, and to remind Jews of our heritage. This Yiddish transliteration of mezuze follows current YIVO Institute for Jewish Research guidelines. There is some evidence that mezuzes originally were intended to keep Lilith out while enforcing monotheism, replacing a tradition of offerings made to Lilith in bowls with circular inscriptions. Lilith is the legendary first partner of Adam who, when she couldn't achieve equality, chose to become a demon. Feminists and lesbians have reclaimed her as a symbol of rebellion against male authority.

[2] brucha = prayer or blessing; mitsve = good deed

[3] The mezuze maker, like many other women, has fallen into the habit of saying "goddess" when she simply means "that awesome power beyond us for which we have no name." She wishes it understood that she is not implying belief in a conscious or protective deity.

[4] chai = life. It is usually written with the Hebrew letters chet and yud, although these are made with only a chet. Originally an accident, a friend expressed the opinion that the yud was used in the word chai as a masculine identifier, so it's now with intention that there is no yud on the mezuzes we make.

[5] Danzig, an independent city-state in 1939, is now Gdansk, Poland.

THE VILDE CHAYA
AND CIVILIZATION[1]

She says, "Civilization is a brick. Everyone knows that, silly.
A brick, a pipe, sheet music and probably sheets. Definitely
sheets."

The Vilde Chaya starts humming:
I come from a country of linen sheets
where tears collect in the shining crease
and you are tucked away from me...

"But let's get back to the bricks," she says. "Out here sometimes I stub my toes, usually it's a rock, but now and then, an
old brick piece. Are there cities rotting beneath me, then? I laugh
and laugh. I dig my teeth into the flesh of trees, I pretend I am
a woodpecker searching for grubs and then I slowly move my
tongue up and down the bark and then my hips—trees really are
a lot more fun than bricks, aren't they?

"Would you like some tea?

"Oh, you think I'm too crazy to eat and drink, that I'd serve
you piss mixed with rain? I just might. For spite. That I might
never appear contrite before the eyes of the law.

"The law.

---

[1] Vilde Chaya is Yiddish for wild beast, something Jewish mothers warn
their daughters against ("Comb your hair—you want to look like a vilde
chaya?")

35

"You know men think that what makes a jew a jew is the law, and women don't have minds of their own, but I am a Vilde Chaya and I know what makes a jewess is a large round mole beneath her left breast. It's the mark of Lilith, her burning fingertip copping a feel of baby flesh as she flees, driven from our cribs.

"I know. I saw her. Well so did you, but you're too prissy to remember. I bet you live in a brick house, I bet you run your hands over your brick patio and praise god for letting you be if not wealthy, well-off. Everyday the men say, 'praise god I'm not a woman' and everyday the women say, 'praise god I own a brick' and they stick their bricks in the fireplace and warm their feet beneath the linen sheets. Women are quite smart you know even if they must have their patios, their walkways, their brocade.

"I know what it means to have womanly art and it's obscene. I am a jew and wild and I bleed and the ants come and lick the trail of my blood. Come closer little ants—and I eat them! They're full of my own blood and we make a perfect circle.

"You can't really make a circle out of bricks can you? But you can hurl them. Glass breaking sounds like bells. I never take anything from behind broken glass. There's a curse on it.

"Even if it's the curse I put out myself, crossing your own curses is the worst luck and I have only good luck. Night after night I sing with Lilith and we make new words to everything because it is not enough to remember what the rabbis did before us, what fire the scholar or the baal shem lit in the forest. No, it's useless. The real task of a jew is to make it all up again not every generation but every life. And the real task of a womon is to spread her legs and swallow the eternal light of synagogues, rub herself all over the darkness, leave her slime in moist corners where it will divide, multiply and grow ripe."

AN ESCAPED
MENTAL PATIENT

Becky sat in the parlor of a halfway house in Baltimore—a converted Victorian row house in a neighborhood gone sour—and convinced a woman to run away with her. Becky, at fourteen, was the youngest in the house, and the woman, Alice, was old enough to drive and own a car. Becky thought she might be as old as twenty-two.

"I can't stand it here anymore," Becky said, with an air of calculated invitation.

"I know what you mean," Alice said.

Becky doubted it. Surely Alice didn't see an identical man's profile in the window across the fire escape, masturbating. Alice didn't even have a fire escape. Perhaps she meant how the psychiatric nurse who ran the house made them feel like boarders in a 19th century mill town, dependent on her largesse in the midst of their collective unhappy circumstances. The three women and four men placed in her care were unable to protest the loud arguments the nurse had with her alcoholic husband. Or anything else, for that matter.

"So let's split. Go somewhere *else*." Becky emphasized *else*, trying to make it sound like cotton candy.

Alice hesitated, checked the polish on her fingernails, which she hoped was the same color as Marilyn Monroe's. "Where?"

"Why do we have to have a destination? Wouldn't it be cool to get in your car and drive until we were too tired to drive anymore?"

"And then what?"

"We'd sleep."

"I don't know." Alice was on the edge of whining. "It's cold out, and I'm supposed to be at work tomorrow."

"You like your job?"

"No."

"Do you ever call in sick?"

"Not so far."

"I have a lot of change saved up. You can call from wherever we get to."

This made Alice giggle, and she covered her mouth with her small hands. "We'll rob your piggybank and run away?"

"We are mental patients—we might as well enjoy it once in awhile."

"We're being rehabilitated." Alice didn't sound convinced.

"The operative word is 'being'—we're not rehabilitated yet, are we?" Becky picked at a thread in the armchair, trying not to sound overly eager.

"What do you think we should take?" Alice stood up, smoothed her skirt with her hands.

"Blankets," Becky said, after the moment of hesitation during which she realized her power and luck.

Alice looked up the staircase. No one had been listening. No one seemed to be around. "But no liquor."

"I don't drink." Becky saw no need to confess that she had recently been introduced to smoking grass by her first roommate from the hospital. Besides, she'd only done it three times.

"Good. Get a blanket and meet me at my car—you know which one?"

"The green Dodge?"

"I'm parked about half-way down the block. Fifteen minutes."

"Don't chicken out."

"Don't you," Alice said, scratching at a chip of nail polish.

They drove southwest, listening to jazz out of Baltimore on the car radio until it crackled and fizzed into country western. Alice smoked filtered Cools. "Give me one," Becky said.

"You're too young to smoke."

"But I do. They taught me in the clinic—we used to hide in the bathroom behind the hydrotherapy tub that Zelda Fitzgerald was tied into, and the women taught me how to smoke."

"Zelda Fitzgerald?" Alice slid the pack across the bench seat.

"You know, Fitzgerald the writer's wife?"

"I know that. She was at the clinic?"

"That's what they said. The clinic in *Tender Is the Night* is supposed to be modeled after it."

"How do you know so much?"

"Smart, I guess."

"Smartass, I'd say." Alice gave Becky an open-handed punch on the shoulder. Becky grinned, rolled down the window to tap ashes into the night air. She had a quick image of the woman who taught her to smoke—Danielle? Danielle taught her about Zelda Fitzgerald sometime after she explained how she was locked up when her family found out about the back-alley abortion, since she nearly bled to death at a cotillion.

Alice liked to drive, and turned up the radio to ward off sleep. When she couldn't push herself anymore, they turned off the highway into a small Virginia town with a train station. It was cold, colder than they'd thought it would be, too cold to sleep in the car. Their blankets were gauze thin, meant to be light covering in the steam heated tenement, and they didn't have enough money for a hotel. They'd start to sleep and then shivering would knock the possibility of rest out of them. Alice would run the car motor carefully for a few minutes at a time, since they knew all about carbon monoxide poisoning from their individual careers as would-be suicides.

They meant to live through the night. Alice got out and went into the train station. Or maybe the train station was locked, and she walked around it, blowing on her movie red fingernails. They slept in bits, breaking off private fragments of the night for comfort.

Becky remembers the smell of cigarette smoke, when cigarettes smelled good, were the smell of nights and runaways and jazz. For a moment, she wishes she had a cigarette again. In midlife, Becky remembers the lights of the cities passing that first cold night, but her memory is a long flickering celluloid reel of the lights of cities she's passed. After all, she had been a child in a mental hospital who made herself a promise: *When I get out, I'll go down every street to see what's on it, I'll travel every road in every state.*

Still Becky insists she remembers the sensation of that specific dark, behind which families closed their doors on the highways of 1964. Although Becky instigated their flight, Alice had to take up the adult role by the time they stopped, be the one responsible for them. She believes that Alice threw up in the railroad station bathroom, from cold and fear. But Becky doesn't remember being particularly afraid, trying to sleep in the back seat of the car, despite how the cold came in under her skin with its switchblade open. She was prepared to suffer for this, a crazy girl on the lam. Alice drove around in circles once an hour to get them warm. The sun came up enormous behind Becky's eyelids; she dreamt the sunrise, the orange globe ringed in red, the brittle sun of February.

She remembers the dream, the night, the cigarettes, the train station. She knows the sun rose because of her dream.

Once it was dawn, they were excused from attempting sleep. Every house on the road was illuminated in its unfamiliarity. They cruised through the town, where they saw milkmen in white uniforms making their morning deliveries from dairy trucks. Becky took in the children going to school, the men coming down to the train station, the bank clerks and grocery store cashiers, the women with their hair in curlers walking from house to house. The opening up of day, the way time unhinges life and lets it out into the street—and she was not part of any of these people's lives. She was invisible to them, something they could not account for. The town encouraged their invisibility, hoping that the slight disturbance she made, she and her companion, would never be something they had to acknowledge.

The townspeople got their wish. Alice did not drive on to Memphis, Mobile, Natchez or New Orleans. She turned around and drove back to Baltimore. They each believed the other had had enough, which was easier than admitting their individual longings for the fragile shelter of the halfway house. Alice was pouting and Becky was disappointed, but neither of them could have begun to say why.

When they were back in Baltimore, Becky found ten dollars in her back pocket. Perhaps with ten dollars they could have rented a room, but they didn't know how to present themselves to a desk clerk. Or perhaps Alice knew that Becky was going to turn out to be a lesbian and was afraid to take a room with her, afraid to pose as sisters or cousins, driving south for, let's say, their grandmother's funeral. There's a plausible story. Becky was at least as smart then as she is now, she could have invented it if she had been ready to convince Alice. But they didn't get a motel room. They tried to keep warm inside the car, attached to being the strangers who pass through, outside of houses, outside of warmth, outside of family.

Becky noticed how the world belongs mostly to animals after dark, how the animals—raccoons and deer, rats and opossums and skunks—appear to have no idea of inside/outside, of finding comfort in cages or locks. In big cities, of course, night workers and restless people, mostly men, a few prostitutes, thieves and insomniacs, cops and students and artists, homeless, frightened, angry people are all out, changing the night. But in whatever small town she and Alice had landed back then, they were the announcement of a turning tide: *Watch out, citizens, the mental hospitals are emptying, the crazy will wander; the economy will turn and turn again, grinding. People who cannot stand the pressure, people who are fighting back, will show up in the railroad stations, in the doorways downtown.*

One night Becky was one of them, but only for a night, because she was fourteen and Alice drove her back to Baltimore. Let out downtown, since Alice went to work after all, only an hour late. Becky went into a department store and bought a present for a woman she loved, a woman who was still locked up. She thought what nice presents you could buy for five dollars. For five dollars, you could make a woman behind bars happy. You didn't have to tell her the story of what might have happened to you but didn't in the middle of your adventure. No rape, no accidental death, no accidents at all. Only discomfort, a dream of the sun as a fierce cold inner eye, and a moment of watching the ordinary life of a town from the outside.

Of course Becky was punished for this; the nurse had reported them missing to the police and her psychiatrist. "You have to learn the rules apply to you," her psychiatrist said.

She can't remember the punishment anymore than she can remember Alice. That she could talk people into things was not lost on her; once, when she was seventeen or nineteen, she convinced a bunch of stoned hippies and gay men to drive from New York's West Village back to Baltimore in a VW van with no heat, for the hell of it, in the middle of winter. For the hell of it, she convinced them, omitting her secret nostalgia to visit the site of her imprisonment and release.

Now she's an ordinary forty-seven-year-old lesbian. She bleeds—on the day she bleeds the most, she is remote and inclined to change her daily habits. She drives through Oakland, bleeding in the heat, a week past solstice. She longs for her lover, and her longing is easily satisfied. She can interrupt her work and they'll have lunch for an hour. She can choose an unusual route and watch the houses waver in the heat and then come into focus—each particular house, each separate life, a whole city, where she lives, an escaped mental patient, with only her little part of the common life. By now, no one would know to look for her.

THE STORY I NEVER WRITE

*So you, what are you crying about? Everything comes around again hard. Even with whatever a rural dyke could want—a lover who gardens, a golden retriever, wild blueberries for breakfast—*my mind goes up in flames in an instant.

I've been listening to the Berkeley Women's Music Collective song, "Thorazine"—"I was chained to the floor with a needle carrying Thorazine / I had something to say..."[1]

I sit in the red chair by the wood stove, stare out the window and count—four of the women whose bodies I touched, four them were locked up and I make five. There must be something to tell about that. But what?

Last week my lover Kasha said she was reading a book about a holocaust survivor who just last year had gotten herself to write what had happen to her when she was a child. She said, "Sometimes survivors take fifty years to tell their stories; sometimes they die with them."

What happened to you when you were a child?
It doesn't matter
it was a long time ago
I'm a different woman now
I don't care.

---

[1] "Thorazine" by Susann Shanbaum, on *Trying to Survive,* by the Berkeley Women's Music Collective, queer toones Publishing, ASCAP, 1978.

That child
standing under the rotunda at Johns Hopkins
staring up at the two-story statue of Christ
the best I can do for her is the best we can do for our daughters
still: hope she makes it out of the corridor
alive.
I don't remember
I don't write this story
I don't even like to allude to it.
The student nurses were nice
one of them always beat me at cards
she wanted me to know I was too much of a brat.
It was a long time ago in Baltimore
and Baltimore is a dead industrial city.
No one remembers it.

Now I work as a printer in the historical society of a small town by the ocean on the Oregon coast. Next to the museum where I clank away on an old letterpress, there's a cafe with a little style, Andrea's. Maggie's the main day waitress, a woman in her forties with a strong British accent. I've watched her for awhile because she has a bright and bitter energy around her. She has a daughter but no obvious man. She plays a musical instrument. She works hard as a waitress.

Andrea's Restaurant has an art show on the wall, which changes. It changed yesterday. I went in for coffee, to hang out, look across the street and worry about whether my long-distance Oakland lover was going to come see me or not, how to pay the bills, and about politics. Several woven sculptures graced the wall. Two boys were discussing them with Maggie, who had made them. Impressed by her work, I think again, *what is this woman doing here?* As anyone wonders about anyone in this town. I admire her work to her. Then return to pretending to correct the typesetting in front of me.

Maggie has Ella Fitzgerald playing. Andrea's in-laws or parents come in. They ask Maggie if she's been to art school; they think her work is so fine. She says no, she was an occupational therapist, you have to learn about twenty crafts to do that. They ask where she had worked as a therapist.

Meanwhile, I'm thinking to myself—*occupational therapist*—and begin to remember a cage at the top of a building. Something I dreamt? The older people questioning Maggie are on the other side of the room so I don't catch everything they say. But I do hear her say Johns Hopkins, that she left there in 1968.

I scribble on the folder. 1949—that's the year I was born—plus 13 = 1962. I consider it for awhile. I watch Maggie move around the room. Not many customers, 11 a.m. I motion to her. "Did you work at Johns Hopkins in 1962?" She says she got there in May of that year. I say, "I was there then."

She says, "Where did you work?"

"I was a patient. I was thirteen. You worked with me in the ceramics room."

She asks, "What's your last name?" I tell her. "Yes, I remember that name." She looks at me again. "One of the things you do when you leave, you try to forget." She adjusts one of the sculptures on the wall. "Do you remember Jackie?"

I remember someone, but it was eighteen years ago.

She says, "Well, you're doing very well."

I laugh, "I guess so."

"Oh, they called you an 'adolescent adjustment,' they never label anyone that young with anything more than that."

Oh yes they do, I want to say but don't. Maggie gets up, goes back to work. I start to shake. I pay the bill and leave her tip and feel strange about tipping. I go back to the letterpress room, tell the story as best as I can to WillaMae, the museum's dyke CETA[2] artist, and later when we have lunch back at Andrea's (because it serves the only edible food in town), Maggie is more open to us; she puts on old jazz and shimmies around the room while she's serving, but other than that she lets it go and I let it go.

it was eighteen years ago
in Baltimore
which is gone now
a city that set in east.

The afternoon wears on me, and the museum seems confining. At lunch, I talk with WillaMae about emotions and control. I say, "I feel like I'm very emotional."

She says, "You sure don't show it."

And I say, "Funny how the skull encompasses you." I think about feeling and try to feel my way through my thoughts and can't. Way back in memory, I can vaguely make out Maggie's face eighteen years ago, unlined, not bitter or clipped the way it is now. She was sweet then, or at least helpful, showing me how to make a blue ceramic vase from a mold. The vase was on my grandmother's TV in New York until my grandmother died, and I keep thinking about that vase and my grandmother and Maggie.

The upstairs of Phipps Clinic starts to come into focus: the attendants bringing your ward of patients to occupational therapy in the elevator. Not everyone—only the ones who no one thinks will use the pointed wood of a paint brush to skewer an eye.

[2] Comprehensive Education and Training Act—an employment initiative legislated under Carter that Regan put an end to in the early 1980s.

Different rooms are apportioned for the various craft categories, and at the end of the room where a bearded man teaches painting, a sun porch looks out over the tenements. You can stand out there, five stories up, and pretend you're climbing on monkey bars if an attendant doesn't catch you. But you are a monkey in a cage. People on the streets below stare if they happen to look up.

I turn my head away, because I don't want to stare at her. But on my bulletin board at home I keep a snapshot someone in my family must have taken: myself at thirteen, sitting on the edge of a metal frame bed on East One, Phipps Clinic, in a sparse room with peeling plaster, smiling for the camera as if it were a junior high class picture. And I feel like—I cannot say how I feel. I refuse. *It was a long time ago. The city is dead.*

Riding home tonight with WillaMae, I stare at the fields full of sheep and conjure a memory of my favorite high school teacher, Rita. Once Rita overheard me tell the story of my life to another student in a quick sketch, "…and then I was in a mental hospital for a year when I was thirteen, and then I was in a halfway house in Baltimore in the slums for another year, and then I was kicked out of a Friends' boarding school, and then I came here." Later Rita laughed at me. She said, "You'll have to get over telling people that—it's such an emotional, manipulative thing to do, dear. You're playing for sympathy or shock. It keeps you from having normal relationships. It keeps you in your role, you know, your role-play of mental patient. You're not so crazy."

That shut me up. I started watching whom I told more carefully. I didn't want anyone's sympathy or to manipulate anyone. So I learned never to say, "…and then I was in a mental hospital for a year," until I knew someone really well, and could counter it with: *but see, that was a long time ago, I'm not crazy, it doesn't mean anything, don't let it even scratch the surface of how you feel about me.*

Now I turn off my typewriter and weep. I lean against it, sobbing. At first I want my grandmother back. Then I start to cry. "You fucking bitch, you fucking bitch." I dig my fingernails into the grain of wood on my desk. "I'm so angry." I will tell you the student nurses were nice, not that they tied me into a chair to set my hair, saying, "You'll thank us for this, it will make you feel like a woman." They too were victims, passing on being a victim. Personal anger is such an indulgence. Women are taught not to indulge in anger anymore than we should indulge in cream; it will ruin our figures, it will ruin our faces. We must save face.

I am so angry about being afraid to tell you. The disapproval, the closing down of a woman you love, and whom you want to love you—this ties you up, ties you to the ground, keeps you down as much as Thorazine. And I've walked around New York so pumped full of Thorazine my joints froze, my body rashed, my vagina turned neon red. I couldn't remember anything except, in the back of my brain, if I ever got home, I would kill myself right, so that wouldn't happen to me again—and I know that careless gynocidal chemical brutality can sometimes be little compared to what we have done to each other for them, in order to win approval from those who have power...

mother to daughter
woman to woman
lover to lover
friend to friend
O you, you're getting personal again
it's not like...

It's not like the men didn't rape you with Freud every way they knew how. I remember one of the Phipps doctors—a giant, self-satisfied man—observing a painting I'd done in occupational therapy, in which there were two mountain peaks. "Hmmm," he said without looking at me. "Clearly you have a regressive fixation on your mother's breasts here." I was very upset. I went to my psychiatrist. I said, "What did he mean?" My psychiatrist knocked the ashes out of his pipe and said, "I wasn't ready to talk about that with you yet." He laughed like it was joke.

What's the joke? I didn't say. He wanted me to get the point: (A) If I paint mountains they'll say they're breasts; (B) It's wrong to paint mountains or breasts, but they'd write in my chart that I was displaying signs of health if I painted trees (I started painting trees); (C) It's regressive, and hardly anything is worse than a thirteen-year-old regressive throwing her emotions around, wanting breasts somewhere in her fantasy. I lay awake thrashing in my bed. My thoughts were teeth, grinding each other: why do they think it's not regressive if a woman wants a penis, why isn't it regressive to want your father, who says it's the right way, why, why did they do this to me.

Years later my mother went to visit the psychiatrist, to talk about old times. He said, "I was just a young resident then, we didn't know a lot, I would have done things differently. But I couldn't have done so badly. Your daughter never went back in again, did she?"

Too many stories clot in my veins. I want to write something—good—about having been a mental patient in a mental hospital in a big city the whole year I was thirteen. Good—that is, linking it up with lovers' experiences:

Lois, who stayed straight, had shock therapy and used to say, "All the plots of the movies are gone, but why I stay with Richard is because he came to the hospital every day and read to me from the newspapers. Even though I didn't hear a word of what he said, he came every day." I bought that for awhile because I knew what it meant. Still I hoped she would realize she had already paid back more than she ever owed him. Last night I read in the *Lesbian Insider,* "Straight women who are locked up get lots of visitors. Lesbians don't."

Mary, who couldn't bear it after her lover of five years left her, got drunk and went to a motel on the Jersey shore, started to carve her lover's name on her arm. Her friends came and locked her up. She was lucky and only had to stay in the hospital two weeks. She survived both the hospital and the fact that her friends couldn't, or wouldn't, imagine any alternative. She rolled up her sleeve to show me with a swagger, flexing the muscle by habit. But when I put out my hand to touch her scar she winced. "Don't," she said, covering her skin, changing the subject.

Sharon. She did not escape drugs or shock therapy or psychosurgery or the judgment of lesbians who thought that if her karma had been in shape those things wouldn't have happened to her. Before her pain, I felt like someone who had survived a camp relatively intact compared to someone who had come out terribly changed, tortured, left furious and broken. I thought it was up to me to fix her life because I understood what had happened to her. Because I had seen the place on the CAT scan where they burned holes in her brain. Because we were lesbians who could do anything, change the actual molecular structure of the wound. But I couldn't fix anything, and I began to use what had happened to Sharon to hide what had happened to me.

And Kasha—whose out of control times haunt her still, a woman who folded in upon herself in deep depression, scared of the faces in the grain of her fear, of the incomprehensible demands of the world. She remembers, "—that time when no one knew what I was going through"—and wants me to speak, wants me to talk about it. All I can say is,

it was a long time ago
I don't want to talk about it.

I was a lesbian child born into a straight family, and I did what I needed to leave them, that's all. The worst I thought could happen to me was to die; they taught me differently.

Many things are worse than death. One is to fall into the institution's hands. Another is to come out of a mental hospital submissive, unable to fight back. A third is fighting back in silence. The fourth is breaking the silence and finding the women around you doubtful, accusing, "What was wrong with you in the first place if you fell into their hands?" Or, "There's nothing we can do about it. When a lesbian is crazy, difficult and in pain, we have no way to help her or to provide refuge; it may be she has to go back in again."

Once I heard a story about a lesbian community that took care of a woman who was in trouble in herself, who had been in hospitals before. They decided she did not have to go back. Women who were her friends and women who hardly knew her took turns staying over, being with her in the place she wanted to be. Over months and months of time. I don't know how they worked it out. The rent, the food money, the time, the commitment to persistence. I heard that they did this, that they did it simply, without condescending, without extracting a debt larger than *I hope you will do it for me if I need it and you can.*

I want to believe this. It would be a convenient way to end the story I can't write about myself anymore tonight because it brings back too many hallways with danger on every side and me that child shielding against it, against the dead women and the dead self in that fear, against the suicide, the remembrance of feeling *there is nothing worth waiting for*, brought back to me today by accident in a cafe on the coast. The circles life makes sometimes shatter me, time falls apart, what I want is never what I think I want and what I get is not satisfying me. In an instant I can be caged again.

After all that starts to stir, hope seems like splinters of glass stuck into both my knees and I don't care what happens to me. Too much comes back, too much has happened to too many lesbians that will never be told. I am too angry and I have no purpose or direction for the anger. I feel very tired and very alone.

I tell myself, *It happened a long time ago.*

THE ORDER OF THINGS

Becky takes the bus from Northampton to Manhattan to visit her mother, Deborah Kaplan, when Deborah comes up from the Caribbean every November for her birthday. Deborah thinks it's amusing, to have inverted the order of things; while New Yorkers begin to fidget and disperse in search of warmth when the first real cold snickers at them, Deborah takes her few winter things out of mothballs and up she comes to see the shows.

Bernie divorced her six years ago, and she'll be damned if he's the only one who gets to enjoy life anymore. She saves up her alimony. "I'm never going to be rich," she laughs, and leaves her elementary school librarian job behind for Thanksgiving weekend (not so far behind that she neglects to fill her suitcase with children's books unavailable in San Juan). Deborah takes a hotel room in the theater district. It's not a luxury room, but a good one, in a nice hotel, with a firm mattress and room service. She tries to avoid paying hotel prices, $2 for a damn cup of coffee, but it's nice to know she could order it just by picking up the phone.

Becky, her only daughter, stays with her, usually for a single night—they see a play, have dinner, sleep in the adjoining beds, maybe shop a little the next day before Becky goes back to Northampton. Deborah has learned to suggest bookstores rather than searching for nice winter skirts at Lane Bryant. Becky is twenty-five now, living the life of a lesbian community activist in the middle of the '70s, engaged with movements and distributing women's films. Clearly Becky's not big on skirts. It seems none of them are anymore.

One of Deborah's brothers-in-law works for the New York tourism bureau, so he gets them theater tickets to an otherwise sold-out drama after which Deborah says of the playwright, "He understands women so well for a man," because the grown woman in the play longed for her father to the point of weeping on a darkened stage. Plays like this embarrass Becky with their watery, self-congratulatory treatment of popular themes, but she has the realization, an epiphany of sorts, that her mother still yearns for Becky's grandfather, who died of a stroke when she was less than a year old.

What motivates straight women is something of a mystery to Becky, yet through Deborah she's been given another clue. She usually thinks of her family like a rash: something private you'd like to ignore that itches, spreads beneath your clothes, something that takes a change of climate to get over. Becky does not long for her own father—she's in the revolutionary phase of believing that when the women come to power (any moment now), they will have to use extreme measures in dealing with the men, and considers the images of fathers and brothers as a series of romantic inventions. She currently admires the idea of re-education camps.

But she likes New York—she was born there, and the insomniac, print-driven energy of the street quickens her. *This is where real life is, maybe the only place.* She knows she gets this idea from her mother, who can't wait to get off Puerto Rico, at least for these five days a year. Besides, her mother has a boyfriend, a married investment banker, whom she met in a casino one night when he was in San Juan on a business trip. Becky knows they see each other at least once during her mother's trips, though Thanksgiving weekend is of course problematic for him. Boyfriend seems as infantilizing a word as the one she has to use, girlfriend, to describe her own attachments. Suddenly Becky gets that outside of marriage, all women's sexual encounters are linguistically trivialized. She doesn't say this to her mother, though.

Once or twice they've tried conversations about men. Deborah cannot understand why Becky can't manage to get along with them.

"They think they're the center of the universe, Mom."

"Of course they do, dear. But I just laugh at them."

"And they don't get mad at you?"

"Oh, I never tell a man what I'm laughing about. It's one of the tricks you learn."

Becky remembers this discussion when she goes to visit her mother at the Sheraton. In the last several years, her mother's face has begun to show the beating the tropic sun gives out; this year she seems to have compressed and hunched in a few inches. Becky's reaction wavers between fear and compassion, which is probably what her mother feels when she looks at her—fat, flannelled, butch. *We have photographs in our minds of exactly how our parents, children, friends should look, full-size boardwalk cutouts into which we keep trying to insert the faces of the people we actually see,* Becky realizes, waving away her mother's cigarette smoke.

"I'm glad you could come down to see me, dear," Deborah says, shifting her cigarette to her other hand, and leaning in for a quick peck at her daughter's cheek.

"My pleasure, Mom," Becky says, trying to mean it. She's angry at her mother. She's angry at women who choose men over women, boys over girls, something left over about her brothers' privileges. She goes to meetings four or five nights a week, and in those meetings they discuss causes and strategies. Which came first, the oppression of women or oppression by race? "Money," someone else says, "it starts with money." *What is power*—Becky asks herself during the five hour bus ride to New York, her vision caught in the bare brown autumnal limbs that try to insinuate hieroglyphic answers in a tangle of directions—*where does power originate?*

One night a meeting was canceled and Becky stayed home, watching *Laverne and Shirley* on the black and white TV that someone who was moving out of town sold her for $20. She liked it so much she began to wish more meetings were canceled. Then she analyzed her desire to be diverted from revolutionary activity, which, she had to admit, was not changing the world quite as quickly as she expected. She thought the minute they explained it to women, what had happened to them, how they'd been duped, women all over the world would rise up, leave their men and join the movement.

It can get cold in New York in November, the first winds picking wet garbage off the street and turning it to sharp blocks of sleet that tear around the concrete towers. Becky's mother never wears pants; Becky's grandmother said a lady never wore slacks out of the house, and was scandalized the night she realized Becky had gone to the Waldorf Astoria (to visit a high school friend in town for college interviews) in jeans. It does not seem to Becky, watching her mother shiver on Eighth Avenue while trying to hail a cab, that stockings are any kind of protection against the weather.

Becky remembers stockings, garter belts and girdles. When she came home after her first suicide attempt, they gave her Thorazine, which made her fat and sluggish, as if she had a swollen, coated tongue not only in her mouth but in her brain. She was only thirteen, and she was stockpiling pills for the next attempt, but no one knew that. Deborah was paying more attention to her daughter's social life because the psychiatrists were accusing her covertly, and while she knew enough to resist "blame the mother," still, wasn't she partly to blame? Deborah encouraged Becky to diet, showed her how to secure the nylon mesh at the top of the stockings in the doodad straps that hung down from the girdle—a button over which the doubled stocking top is secured with a metal hook. Later the doodad straps, buttons and metal dig into your thighs, and the girdle rides up, cutting off circulation to your legs.

You are at someone's bar mitzvah, because after all, you're thirteen and the boys are having their parties at hotels with swans carved out of ice that melt quickly on the outskirts of San Juan. The boys make fun of you because you've gotten wide and you have lipstick on your teeth. You would make fun of yourself if you could because lipstick feels greasy and mask-like. You are stoned from the Thorazine, and you have some kind of powder on your face that your mother showed you how to put on but which grates like a layer of sandy leather. Somebody's father, perhaps your own, gave you a drink which now is making you feel like throwing up on the shoes of whomever it is you're dancing with. The dance floor full of thirteen year old boys and girls doing the twist amid flashing lights makes you think of the paintings you've seen of hell. When you get to the bathroom, you put your head between your legs until your mother comes to find you and you convince her you're only not feeling well, "Can we go home, please?" Your mother is flustered, but she doesn't hiss, *Will you never fit in?* She is pained; she clenches her purse as tightly as her lips. She wants you to be like all the other girls your age who seem to be having such a nice time, and look so pretty in their new dresses. Perhaps she sincerely wants your happiness, though you have no way to tell her what that would consist of, and she has no way to help you speak.

Becky and Deborah are at the Stage Deli about an hour before Becky's bus goes back to Northampton.

"Mom, I was thinking recently how it must have been for you and Dad…" Becky pauses, fiddling with putting more mustard on her rye bread.

"What do you mean, honey?" Deborah lights a fresh cigarette. She's smoked all her life, except, she says, when she was pregnant. Not that they knew, then. But during pregnancy cigarettes nauseated her, a fortuitous thing.

"I was thinking how it must have been to have a child who kept trying to kill herself, how painful it must have been." Again Becky pauses, looking directly at Deborah for the first time during the meal. "I'm sorry."

Deborah puts her hand over Becky's. "Oh, honey." She takes a long pull of smoke. "You don't have to apologize to me. I'm sorry for what I did to you."

"What do you mean?" Becky frowns. She wants her own recent revelation to get more space. Although she intends not to have biological children, she's taken an interest in the daughters of her friends. Watching them, she has found herself protective, adult. How would she feel if one of them became persistently self-destructive? What if Helen's daughter Magda slit her wrists? With that thought, she looked into the scenes of her own childhood drama as if she were looking at a snow-globe, and saw the stricken grown-ups attending the child—her own parents, miserable and powerless over Becky's hopelessness.

"I'm the one who should apologize," Deborah says. "The doctors said I should try to make you take more interest in being like the other girls."

"You mean the make-up and the girdles?"

Deborah sighs. "We didn't know what you girls know since the women's movement. I really thought I was doing the best thing for you. I can see now it was wrong."

"Oh, Mom." Becky pauses. She looks at her mother and her mother looks back. They have extremely different faces—different coloring, different eyes, different length of nose and chin. Becky takes after her father more, or one of Deborah's sisters.

"Well, I am sorry about it. Not all girls are the same," Deborah says, snuffing out the cigarette on her plate.

"No, we're not." Becky resists the impulse to correct her mother, *Can't you say women, Mom, women?* Instead she squeezes her mother's hand. "Thanks," she says.

"I don't want you to miss your bus."

"I won't, Mom. Let me get the check."

"Don't be ridiculous. Age before beauty, don't contradict your mother. I always say I'm never going to die rich."

"Well—OK." *Is it good revolutionary form to let your mother pay for you?* To like that your mother still pays for you? "Have a good time while you're here." She pauses, and opens a smile in her mother's direction. "Thanks, Mom."

Her mother smiles backs, "It was good to see you, sweetheart."

Becky is elated in the cab, and almost skips her way through Port Authority bus terminal. All these years she had been so anxious about talking to her mother, as if, should they really acknowledge her childhood, the Earth would split and grind them both in its terrible crystal gears. Usually her mother refers to that time as "when you were so sick," and changes the subject. But her mother understood how Becky had suffered for being a girl. *Well, maybe she doesn't understand it, exactly, but she can see it. She said she was sorry.* Becky is amazed. *She apologized. We apologized to each other. I'm a grown-up now.*

The woman who founded the Woman's Center in her town happens to get on the same bus with her.

"My mother told me she was sorry today."

"Oh?" the woman says, who's only an acquaintance, a straight woman who likes to see things get done.

"She apologized for pressuring me into a role—you know, make-up and dates—when I was an adolescent," Becky says, sensing that the abridged version is called for.

"That sounds like a good thing for you two."

"It was," Becky says, watching the Art Deco arches of the Chrysler building, her favorite skyscraper, disappear.

FAUST

The summer after Becky was expelled from the Friends boarding school for being unsuitable, she traded families with one of her second cousins—he went to live in California with her parents, and she got his bedroom in Princeton.

Becky was particularly fond of the Princeton second cousins. Cousin Evelyn at forty was one of those women who never stopped shining after the men came home from World War II. She exuded a daytime glamour, the clean enthusiasm of a USO entertainer, which charmed adults. She also took a genuine interest in children, unlike many of her female family peers, who, having glimpsed engagement with the world and been pressured to renounce lives of broad influence, were often confounded by the presence of their own offspring.

Becky's mother Deborah was one of the confounded—when Becky had tried to kill herself at thirteen, her mother, after getting through the shame ("the family will blame it on me") and anger ("what did I do wrong, anyway?"), was genuinely perplexed. She'd asked Becky if everything was all right, and Becky said yes. Why would she lie to her mother? The doctors said Becky couldn't live at home anymore—were they really that poisonous, that unreliable? The Friends boarding school outside of Baltimore had seemed like a reasonable solution, although, god knew, it was more than they could afford. Now that she was not "invited" back, what were they going to do? Thank goodness cousin Evelyn agreed to take Becky for the summer. Last summer Becky had barricaded herself in the bathroom and insisted she'd slit her wrists if they made her come live with them again. It wasn't good for the boys to be around that. Easier to tell them that Becky was sick, and had to live in a different climate. When they were older ,Deborah could figure out a better explanation.

Oblivious to her mother's angst, Becky cosseted herself in her own loss. Alone in the New Jersey dark of her cousin Brad's bedroom, she tortured herself over being severed from the first cohort she'd had outside the mental institution. Before the Friends school, the last time she'd had intimates her own age she'd been eleven. When she was locked up, her psychiatrist told her, or the nurses told her, that friendships you make "inside" don't last, and she'd taken that advice as seriously as she could. But the only thing they'd warned her about when she left was to keep her institutionalization a secret. No one uttered a word of warning on the impermanence of adolescent relationships, on the possibility that your ties can be broken by events beyond your control.

No doubt she was kicked out of the Friends school because of Julia's father finding their letters. Julia was a day student from a prominent Maryland Quaker family; she and Becky were different as willow and oak. Julia was tall, thin, blonde and everyone admired her; she smiled good-naturedly at the boys whom, of course, her father wouldn't let her date, and besides, she had to practice. She played the piano. Julia was in training to be a concert pianist, had already performed once with a local orchestra. Becky would linger with her in the practice room, which was next to a hill of grass, alternately staring at Julia's hands and the motion of the weeds, as if the music, not the wind, moved them.

They sat next to each other in class—their attraction must have started during discussions of *Portrait of the Artist as a Young Man*—because they were both girls who thought of themselves as artists, who held the secret word "genius" like chocolate under their tongues until it melted, and they recognized each other in their sweetened prides. Soon Julia started using Becky's room to hang out when she had a free period or if her parents were going to be late picking her up.

Becky read one of Pearl Buck's novels and was inspired by it to suggest that they call each other "sister," as a way of showing their deep regard for each other.

"Sister, I missed you," Becky said when Julia showed up in her room after being out with a cold.

Julia blushed—she was very pale and the blood branched up through her skin, visible even through her hair. "I missed you too, Sister." She ran her long fingers over Becky's.

Becky thought she might faint. She paused too long, struggling to bring herself to caress Julia's hand. Julia turned to her book bag, pulling out the letter she'd written while she was home sniffling. "Read it later," she whispered, leaning in close, although no one else was around. "I have science class in five minutes."

Fifteen and flowery, Becky held the letter up to her cheek, ran her finger over its edges, put it down, picked it up again, before she broke the sealing wax that closed the flap. "Dearest sister, before you, the only one I could talk to was the spotted goat I raised on a bottle after his mother died..."

Becky started a reply that ran to 104 pages—of course, some of the pages only had a word or two on them ("Courage!" or "Dream!") written wide and sideways. On paper she confessed her desires—not about caressing, although she did write, "I long to be gentle with you." But what she concentrated on getting across was how she burned to achieve something important. She was determined to be great, as great as Julia was on the piano. Sometimes at night she felt she could stretch her hands out to touch the bowl of the dark, rip it open, and make wonder rain down on the world. All this she trusted to Julia.

About two months from the end of the school year, the head master called Becky into his office. He had a stack of the letters in front of him. "Do you recognize these?"

Becky didn't need to answer.

"I've warned you before. You think you're so special. But we can't allow you to go around influencing innocent girls like Julia."

"Influencing?"

"I don't want to hear your opinion about this. We thought this school could have a good effect on someone with your history, but I think we made a mistake. Your people are stubborn, and I've had about enough of you. You stay away from her, do you hear? No more letters. Your teachers have been instructed to separate you in class."

"But what does Julia want?" She held one hand tightly in the other, as if she were at the dentist and the Novocain wasn't working.

"Julia wants what her father wants. I told you," he said, wagging a stubby finger in her face. "You better shape up. Now get out of here."

"Can I have the letters back?"

"May I," he corrected. He held the stack between his hands and tore them in half, which caused him visible effort, enough to make his cheeks red and his hands shake. He made smaller piles to tear the halves into quarters. This actually relieved Becky. "Still want them?"

"Yes."

He threw them at her and stood up. "I don't want to see a scrap of paper on this floor when I come back. Pick them up and get out."

Neither Julia nor Becky spoke about the letters after a quick whispered "I'm sorry" as they passed each other leaving morning meeting. They communicated with their eyes when they could, and found the moment on Tuesday and Thursday afternoons when no one noticed Becky going into the practice room about half an hour after Julia.

"I could teach you to play," Julia said.

"I'd like that." Becky's hands were small, her fingers short. She sat next to Julia on the piano bench, and Julia explained how to do a basic scale, modeling the hand positions.

"Now you try."

Their arms brushed against each other. A spasm snapped through Becky's nerves.

"Are you all right?"

"Fine."

Becky was not exactly a natural, but Julia was patient with her; they sat together for half an hour or so grazing each other's arms, putting their hands on fingers to get the feel of the keys, before Julia would say, "I have to practice now," and Becky would move to her chair by the window, where she watched the grass undulate in the green melody. They got away with it for about three weeks before the science teacher found them.

"I was teaching Becky how to do scales," Julia explained, mustering her most cheerful expression. Becky knew enough to let Julia make their excuses.

The teacher looked at them softly. He'd heard someone practicing scales, and he knew Julia's skill went far beyond what he'd heard. It seemed harmless enough, sweet, even, but he couldn't allow them to keep at it. "Sorry, girls," he said.

It was only three weeks to the end of the school year; the headmaster waited and sent the expulsion notice to Becky's home to avoid a scene—the girl had advocates; the history teacher and school nurse both opposed him when he'd tried to expel her earlier.

When Becky got the news at her parents' house in Santa Monica, their cousin Evelyn's husband Paul happened to be visiting. He took Becky out to breakfast and explained the plan for her to spend the summer with him and Evelyn, so long as she didn't mind Brad using her room. She no longer thought of her room as "her room"—her brothers had colonized it with football detritus and snorkeling gear—and being close to Evelyn was better than going to Disneyland, as far as Becky was concerned.

"You see, you're more resilient than people think," Paul said. "I've always been on your side, kid."

Becky had no idea what that meant, but she was used to adults who wanted to be both cool and kind, so she smiled at him and finished eating her eggs.

Because Princeton is a college town, the local high school had a summer course in great books, in which Becky enrolled. She was the youngest person in the class, but only by a year. The teacher was gratified to have a willing group for the *Iliad, Odyssey* and *Faust*—twelve pupils who always did their homework. What Becky liked was being treated as if she had a grown-up mind. At the Friends school, everyone was always surprised when she decoded Joyce's Catholic symbolism or decided Hemingway was overrated. One of her classmates had confessed that she thought Becky was making it up when she said she got all A's (or the equivalent of A's, since the Friends school used an arcane number system), because fat girls will say anything to make themselves look good.

Becky bicycled back and forth to the great books course. Bicycling was more exercise than she was used to, and, flushed, straining uphill on the way back to Evelyn's house, she would stop at a particular rock and let the blood even out in her temples.

One day, perched on a stone outcropping to rest, she suddenly felt as if the top of her head were lifted off, and, once open, touched a brilliant cloud, which was no ordinary cloud, but the motion of living thought. The exposed nerve of her brain quavered, plucked by the hand of a cold cosmic wind. An unfamiliar ecstasy twined itself with the pulse, with the pulp, of her veins. In that moment of revelation, she understood that consciousness was a continuum—that the rock she sat on participated in consciousness as much as she did, spoke to her then in the manner of its being, in its own rock voice. High above her, and yet at her same height, was a form of pure idea/energy which she could only dip into—open up to—in the breakthrough moment.

Becky got up, remounted the bike. But being distracted, she immediately fell and skinned her knee. Evelyn was handy with Band-Aids and peroxide, generous with the curve of her arm and sympathy. Becky wanted to tell Evelyn about her idea, her experience of moving outside her body in the realm of beatific thought, but couldn't find the way to say it. She talked about *Faust* instead.

"You're enjoying that?"

"It's so neat—he makes a bargain with the devil that the devil can take his soul if he's ever satisfied."

Evelyn sighed, "Sweetie, that's beyond me. Why would someone want to not be satisfied?"

"Because he wanted to know everything. And there's always more to learn."

"I suppose there is." Evelyn smiled at her, and Becky realized she was being indulged, which humiliated her in an odd way more than having all those letters thrown at her in tiny bits.

"But listen to how it goes." Becky leafed through the book on the table in front of her. "'If I should ever say to the moment, stay, thou art so fair—then you may claim my soul then and there.'"

"It's very dramatic." Evelyn gathered the ingredients for the new recipe she was trying. "But honey…" she concentrated for a moment on Becky, taking in her excitement. "No one can sustain a moment of satisfaction. If we're lucky, we can look back on them and feel good about the moments in our lives."

"I don't want to settle for a string of little happinesses." Becky grimaced and thumbed the edges of the pages.

"Trust me—you might think of it as bourgeois now, or settling, but happiness is seriously underrated. And, you know, knowledge doesn't come only from books." Evelyn ruffled Becky's hair, which thrilled Becky, though she shrugged as if it annoyed her. "Some things we can only learn with our hearts, even if that sounds trite to you now." She turned to look for her chopping knife. "What happens to your Faust, anyway?"

"Oh—he falls in love."

"See what I mean? And does the devil take him?"

"No, heaven has pity on him and sends down a rain of rose petals. That part's pretty cheesy."

"You may be among the first to call Goethe cheesy—at least in my house. But we have other fish to fry, as they say. Would you help me chop onions?"

Several weeks later, Becky's mother flew east to take Becky for an interview at an experimental school run by Holocaust refugees who had developed a philosophy around channeling adolescent sexual energy without being authoritarian. "This is the last one, Becky," Deborah said. "If you can't get along here…"

But Stone Mountain School was perfect for Becky. Her first week, her roommate Iris said everyone called it Stoned Mountain and passed her a joint. Becky returned the favor by offering amphetamine her mother sent, courtesy of diet doctors. They shared a narrow room in a group of four on the second floor of the north side of the main building—an imposing stone mansion built and abandoned by some New England robber baron. The dining room was almost directly below them; most of their classes were down the hill, although the art studio, presided over by a gray-haired woman who had once taught at the Bauhaus, was uphill, hidden in a grove of trees.

Everyone at Stone Mountain seemed as displaced as Becky— in the four rooms on her hall were a nineteen-year-old alcoholic determined to finish her senior year; two African American girls, one on scholarship from rural Alabama and one the daughter of a popular singer; her roommate, a working-class girl from Detroit, also on scholarship, who wanted to be an artist and found Stone Mountain through a newspaper ad; a cheerleader who had flunked out of a more prestigious school and was clearly disgusted by her new surroundings; an Italian girl from Queens whose newly divorced mother worked on the grounds crew; a Venezuelan whose father was a diplomat; the kleptomaniac daughter of a naturalist whose books were often on the *Times* best seller list. And they were a fairly representative sample, although the boy's side held a number of athletes (a Harlem Iranian and Thai prince among them) disappointed by the lack of varsity spirit, along with America's youngest MENSA member, just as disgruntled by the cavalier attitude of most Stone Mountain students toward academics.

"But the teachers—" Becky countered, on her way to the art studio.

"Well, the European ones anyway," the MENSA boy said. "They're all right."

Dr. Margaret, the school's German co-founder, was delighted when Becky admitted she'd read *Faust,* even if it was the abridged English translation. "You must come up to my study, and we'll read Goethe together, you and I. I'll translate for you myself."

Becky found this slightly creepy. While she had learned to be polite, she was distrustful of adults, and Dr. M reminded her a little of the witch in the story of Hansel and Gretel. "Come

71

read the *Faust* with me, little girl." It was rumored that Dr. M had studied with Freud in Vienna, which only increased Becky's shiver, although she realized she should be flattered since everyone agreed that Dr. M was a great woman. She hoped that not all great women ended up in darkened rooms above high school dorms in small towns.

"Yah, maybe you want to see this from another angle," Dr. M said, pulling a thick black book out of her bookcase, and wiping off the dust with her sleeve in her darkened study. "Thomas Mann—*Dr. Faustus*. You can tell me what he does with this theme, yah?" Becky, greedy for books pulled out of cryptic libraries, accepted the challenge. But when Dr. M wanted to talk she found excuses to be busy—after all, she was editor of the school newspaper by her third month. She wanted to make a difference, but to girls her own age, not to Dr. M. The diet pills kept her up, thinking, reading, doodling, tinkering with the mimeograph machine and stencils.

The newspaper office was in a small octagonal marble building that had once been a tea house for the manor. Becky got dispensation to work on the newspaper after lights out so long as her grades didn't slip and she was back in her room by midnight, although no one ever checked. Thomas Mann was dense, a thicket of modern and medieval German rendered into an English that could tear at your thoughts like blackberry thorns—none of the silly rhymes of the *Faust* translation that made it easy to skim. Becky was a slow reader, patiently swacking her way through every line.

Mann's *Faust* was not the gnarly medieval alchemist but a 20th century musician; his devil was sophisticated and theologically astute. Becky read in the octagon while an uncomfortable sensation of immediacy suffused her. The Faust character protests that the power a man gets by making a pact with the devil is unnatural, not his own power, and so nothing he can take pleasure or pride from. Mann's devil counters, "If you were a potter before the invention of the kiln, you baked your pots in the sun, a wholly natural way to create. But now that we have the kiln, is your creation less your own from being fired in the intensity of fabricated heat? Not at all—your creations come out stronger, more capable of withstanding elements and time, able to sport lustrous colors unimaginable before."

Becky closed the book. It was February, and the room only had a small electric heater. She stretched and went outside. The stars buckled the cold night into the trees. She remembered something from the play *The Devil and Daniel Webster* about the scrunch of boots on fresh snow, but she couldn't fix the language in her memory. Because she came from a place without much winter, she felt as if she were sneaking some unintended pleasure out of the white field that stretched down in back of the dorms, getting a late night intimation of power no one expected girls to experience. Then she felt someone watching her. She turned her head quickly, but saw only shadows. "Who's there?" she whispered. Her breath froze in the air. A whoosh rolled over her. The first owl she'd ever seen spread its wings a yard wide, sailing in black silhouette before it disappeared into the trees.

Becky exhaled slowly. Then she walked deliberately upstairs, trying to keep down the creak in the old floorboards. The bathroom her section shared had one toilet and an old claw foot enameled tub. In the mornings, they had to be down for breakfast by eight sharp, because at eight sharp the music teacher played the morning selection—Scarlatti usually—and then the doors to the dining room were locked. If you were locked out, you got a demerit before they let you in to eat. The girls were always shoving and yelling at each other to hurry up in the bathroom early in the morning, but after midnight you could sit as long as you liked.

As Becky sat, she experienced another presence in the room. When she looked at the bathtub, a man was sitting on it. Not a man, exactly—the shade of man, she'd have to say. Or the projection of one. He was small, formally and neatly dressed in a dark suit, a derby and a bow tie. He crossed his legs at the knee, steadying himself with a brass-knobbed cane. "Well?" he asked.

"Well what?" Becky said. She had the sensation of wanting to scream, or at least get her roommate. But she couldn't take her eyes off him.

"Are you ready? Are you not convinced?"

"Convinced?"

"Don't be coy. It isn't creation so much as the sensation of creating, the throb of your body in its fervor, that you long for. And, of course, the recognition. We are perfectly ready to negotiate."

Becky blinked. The man shifted his hands on his cane, but kept his gaze steady. "Umm," she said. "It's late, and this doesn't seem like a very dignified place to do business."

"I agree. Shall we say tomorrow night, then?"

"Tomorrow night, in my office."

"Ah, yes. Your office." Had it hissed the last words? Before she could ask any questions, the specter nodded and vanished.

Slipping into her room without waking her roommate Iris, she wondered who he had been—the devil or Thomas Mann. Was it real? *It's funny what amphetamine does to your mind, she thought, before falling asleep.* All night she had the sensation of being too cold, but too tired to get up for another blanket.

The next evening, several of the other writers for the newspaper and Iris hung around the tea house after dinner. Around eight, Becky insisted she needed quiet in order to get any work done and made them leave. She was jittery, walking back and forth over the big tiles that made up the floor. After awhile she became aware of a mass of furry energy mushrooming out of space on the other side of the room. For a moment it was something like a bear, and then turned into a hazily defined, very large poodle. She laughed.

Then she felt a sensation of claws on her shoulders, and her anus tightened involuntarily.

"This is not a laughing matter."

"Are you a dog, then?"

"I am whatever I choose to be. If you don't make the bargain, you will never see the full extent of my dominion."

Becky put her hand on Mann's book. "I understand your dominion."

The presence snorted, not as a human might, but as a bull, preparing to spear the thing that goads it.

Becky relaxed. The length of her days condensed to a small point in the Massachusetts woods, crushed in the demon's hand as if it were turning the carbon of her physical being into diamond. She had never felt so focused.

"Then you are unafraid."

"Fear seems beside the point."

"Good, very good. You are ready?"

The argument about the sun versus the kiln ran through her mind like a fast forwarding tape. What power would she ever have on her own? She had survived two suicide attempts, but that only marked her as Other, along with all the other markers congealing in her body. She wanted more than anything to be taken seriously, to feel and be felt in her strength.

"Get thee behind me, satan," she said out loud, "so that I may be a mask for thee." This struck her as almost silly in its melodrama, but she swallowed her impulse to laugh.

The presence transformed into something like a human shape and tightened its grip on her shoulders. She held out her hand - -

"Becky! Becky!" Iris burst through the door. "You have a long distance phone call—the woman said it was urgent, a matter of life and death."

Becky shuddered and turned to Iris. "What?"

"Someone's on the phone for you in the main house. You better go see what it's about."

Becky turned back to the room, which seemed to her alive with swirling, ghostly mud.

"What are you looking at?" Iris asked.

"Nothing."

"You better hurry."

"OK, OK." Becky grabbed the book and followed Iris through the side door to the pay phones by the mail boxes. "Hello?"

"Becky? It's Julia. I only hope I'm not too late."

"Julia? How did you get permission to call me?"

"I had to beg them."

"What's wrong?"

"It's something that's happening to you. You're in mortal danger. I felt it last night, but tonight I felt it so strongly I couldn't breathe. Are you all right?"

Becky stared at the phone. She saw the wind flatten the grass on the Maryland hill outside the practice room. She remembered how Julia's smile made a lopsided dimple on one side of her face. "You're not going to believe this—"

"I'll believe you."

"I was about to seal a pact with the devil for my soul."

"Did you finish?"

"I don't think so. I—I mean, I didn't really believe it was happening. You know, I thought I was making it up."

"Believe me, Becky, it was real."

"Maybe—I thought it was the diet pills."

"You still taking those?"

"My mother sends them."

"You should tell her to stop. But it wasn't the pills."

"How do you know?"

"I don't know how. I just know. Listen, I can't stay on the phone—"

"I understand." Becky realized she was sweating. The book cover was taking the imprint of her sticky palm.

"Promise me to be careful. Promise me you'll do whatever you can to change what was happening."

"I promise. Can I write you?"

"No, they check my mail."

"I'm sorry."

"It's okay. I —"

"Yeah, me too, Julia."

"Good. But don't make me feel this way again, OK?"

"OK, I promise."

"Listen, I have to hang up. Take care of yourself, Sister."

"Sister—" Becky answered as the line clicked. She sat in the phone booth, staring at the floor. She didn't want to leave the main house, at least until it was light, so she went to her room.

"What was that about?" Iris asked her.

"An old friend of mine. She was worried about me." Becky looked out the window at the tea house.

"Did you tell her you were fine?"

"Yeah. I'm fine. But I think I'll go see if Dr. M is still awake."

Iris turned from her desk to stare at Becky. "I don't even like to go to Dr. M's apartment during the day."

"I know." Becky bit at her thumbnail. "But I just finished a book she lent me, and I wanted to talk to her about it."

"You're weird, you know."

"You just figured that out?"

Iris shrugged and went back to her trigonometry home-work.

As she picked up Dr. M's book, Becky had the brief sensation of flame nipping her hand.

TWO DREAMS

Phyllis dreamed her favorite dreams when she was still Becky, twenty years ago, before she decided to take a name that meant leafy branch (let everyone else call themselves Tumbleweed or Lapis; she meant to keep her new life to herself).

In the first, she follows the magic dog across a tightrope strung between high cliffs. She stretches her arms so wide that wonder enters through her fingertips. She is laughing, one foot in front of the next on a braided rope. Steady, careful—the magic dog is all encouragement. What a thrill this caution is!

Of course they fall. She can still remember that flick of air against her eyeballs, sharp, blue and cool. Wonderful relief—to fall with so much luxury and time in the falling. Time enough to know her own body as the site of sensation. In a dream like this, there is no fear, no splat. There is only waking in a changed skin, a skin that's become one with the pleasure of licking an ice cream sky, her eyes a tongue pressed into the sweetness of daring.

The second is a tidal wave dream: she's had them often, all her life. They come from a childhood intimacy with the beach, learning the seasonal change of high waters pushing against seawalls in storm. Sometimes they mean sex, other times upheaval or a longing for change.

In this particular one, she lives in a small house set on a jutting flat rock halfway down a long ocean bluff. The tidal wave is coming: suddenly she is watching from above, her house shrunk to doll house size. The wave slams over it and recedes.

She walks back in: everything is exactly the same, except washed clean, a few grains of sand glittering on the floor. A voice enters her dream: *You see,* it says, *you are too small to ever be harmed.*

TWO STORIES ABOUT FERRIS WHEELS

i

Becky had a younger maternal cousin, Zach, who had been brain damaged at birth. He was sent to a progressive institution at a fairly young age, but came home often for special occasions. Becky's mother was always fond of this nephew and took him to baseball games, outings everyone said he looked forward to. Once he visited when Becky was a child, and ran around the house switching the lights on and off. He loved the click, the power of the switch, and something about it—maybe knowing that it annoyed others—gave him an air of exhilaration as he rushed from one electrical face plate to another.

The summer Becky was fifteen, he and his mother, her aunt, came to visit Becky, who was staying with relatives on her father's side. They all trundled out to Rye Playground, a popular amusement park in the suburbs north of New York City. Zach wanted to go on the Ferris wheel, but no one wanted to take him. Eventually—perhaps much sooner than eventually because Becky liked the Ferris wheel—she volunteered. It was dark already when they got in the swinging basket; the bar came down across their laps and they were bolted in. Zach became very quiet, unusually still, as the wheel started to turn. He reached for Becky's hand, and she took it.

The Ferris wheel went around once before it stopped. Becky and her cousin were a basket or two past the top, so they couldn't

81

see the structure behind them, only the carnival spread out below. It was starting to rain, summer rain, slow, deliberate, fat drops breaking loose from the dark, turning a stunning silver as they entered the field of colored beams that the amusement park sent up. Zach pointed with his free hand. They watched the big rain come down to them, whispering a story, and the world below seemed far away, receding as if they were on a rocket ride, going somewhere, somewhere else.

Something was wrong and needed to be fixed. Five minutes, maybe ten—time blew off the horizon, steam from a stranger's hot cocoa. Their relatives waved to them from the ground but they didn't care.

Becky saw how relieved everyone was when the wheel creaked forward, depositing them on the platform, although she didn't think her cousin noticed. He was still looking at the sky. A kinship feathered up in her, a connection to everyone who needed to be accounted for but didn't count. And she had a new appreciation for the dark, the rain, the small lights that humans send out to illuminate their situations.

ii

The last time Phyllis went on a Ferris wheel was at the Curry County Fair, the southernmost county fair on the Oregon coast. The fairgrounds were on a field at the edge of the ocean—the only other place she knew with this enormous luxury was the boardwalk in Santa Cruz, which was a crowded, permanent set of attractions on Monterey Bay. But the Curry County Fair only lasted two weeks a year; like other fairgrounds, its stadium and exhibition hall were used for various events in other seasons. It was a rural county, its towns twenty miles apart and sparsely populated in between. Retirees, loggers, forestry types, sheep ranchers, fisher folks, tourist trade personnel made up most of the handful who'd chosen this isolated stretch.

Phyllis and Kasha had a friend nearby who had two young girls, eleven and twelve, and they'd borrow the kids to drive down the coast for the fair. Children are the best excuse for the self-indulgences county fairs require. They saw a whale spouting on the way down—although the migration hadn't begun, neither coming or going being in season then, occasionally a gray whale would stick around the coast, and some orcas had taken up residence in the bay by Port Orford—another friend had watched through binoculars as one of them ate a seal.

They had a different kind of life then, the kind that city women make in the sticks, with weekend days spent gathering mussels at low tide or sitting on the docks in Charleston throwing down the big crab rings baited with fish heads, drinking beer and watching the blue herons which nested across the slough as they waited the twenty minutes between checking the catch. Phyllis spent her lunch hours watching storms come in off the ocean. She and Kasha kept a copy of the tide table in the kitchen and car glove box. They scanned the penny advertiser for local events— the fishwives' salmon fest, the cranberry harvest parade.

Most county fairs had the same trucked-in attractions—a merry go round for the youngest, some frightening looking rides that swung caged adolescents in great arcs, a Ferris wheel, one or two other contraptions, along with a midway where you could throw rings around ducks moving in a tub of water, shoot darts, squirt water into clowns' mouths in order to burst a balloon before anyone else, throw basketballs into an oddly rigged hoop. Someone offered to guess your weight and age.

In the permanent sheds, locals competed for biggest vegetable, best jam, most beautiful quilt, and they took real pleasure in perusing these offerings—once Phyllis even considered entering a peach chutney she'd made in a fit of longing for the taste of something one of her favorite teachers whipped up fifteen years before. In the country, they had time to find canning jars and spend all day stirring peaches and cinnamon. Sometimes the 4-H clubs had exhibits about animal husbandry or natural dyes. The children were patient, and occasionally engaged, as they were dragged through these rustic presentations.

Phyllis didn't take to being jostled the way she did when, at ten, she craved the crash and thump of bumper cars. But every year she persuaded the borrowed girls to go on the Ferris wheel with her. Who wouldn't want to? Of course it's scary—gawky distracted boys who feign interest tend fragile erector set machinery that's hustled from town to town on flat bed trucks traversing potholed roads, and the swing of Ferris wheel baskets gets the remnants of hot dogs and funnel cakes lurching in your belly. The kids balked a little about being strapped so helplessly in.

But Phyllis knew the top—a view over the green fields of Curry County out to sea. She put her arms around the girl on each side. "Girls," she said, "you'll never see anything better. This is the life." The girls rolled their eyes. The sun grazed a path along the waves that concealed the great mammals, still swimming free. That silver swath echoed Phyllis's lover's smile, as if the whole sea grinned for her pleasure as she swung carelessly above the Earth.

STAKING CLAIMS

Sophie and I are sitting at a table in Berkeley with a view of the San Francisco bay. It's only late afternoon, but we're hungry for dinner. We've never been to this restaurant before—it's new, clearly fashionable, with a huge menu of attractive foods.

Only recently am I comfortable to order what I want when I'm with Sophie; I should have had that ease years ago, but our relationship has peculiar pockets of strain left over from its long-distance-romance beginning. Finally I order as best as I can from the wide list, and damn the waitress who hides a snicker at two fat women ordering full dinners at four o'clock in the afternoon.

As soon as the waitress is gone, Sophie starts, as if we have been interrupted in the middle of a conversation about her two current lovers—which we haven't. I've been hoping to talk about politics, catalog shopping, or even the weather.

"They have me in a custody trial, Marge and Bendita. That's what it feels like, a custody trial. Everyone wants a piece of me," Sophie complains. "Shouldn't I be the one who gets custody of myself?"

I'm glad she doesn't include me among her intimate assailants, yet I feel hurt and invisible not to be included. It wasn't only the lack of jobs and Jews in Oregon that inspired me to move 500 miles six months after we'd stopped making love. But I'm not ready to talk about that yet.

The sun is bright, and green cascades off the island hills. I'm looking away from her, to the north, when I say, "Let's imagine you're a country, and you're staking a claim. Where do you stake it?"

I turn back to see her mime driving a stake through her bowels.

"How does that feel?" I ask.

"It hurts, Phyllis," she says, "I think I put it in too deep."

I shake my head. The waitress brings a beer. Something called St. Stans Amber, which I ordered only because I liked the name, but turns out to be delicious. "All right," I say, "go down to the land claim office and register your claim."

"Up," she says, "the land claim office is up here," and she points to her head.

"Okay, up. I'll be the clerk. What's the name of your claim, ma'am?"

"Sophie," she says.

"And what are the boundaries of this Sophie claim you've staked out?"

She draws a little box about two feet out from her, in the air.

"Describe them please, ma'am. This is being written down."

"My flesh, my bones, what's inside me, and five feet around me."

"And what does the inner country look like? Desert, rocky, mountainous, dry, bodies of water, plains?"

"Oh," she says, and visibly expands with the sensation of interior landscape.

The waitress puts down a plate of small fried calamari rings and another of fried mozzarella. I had hesitated before ordering the mozzarella, but I love it if it's done right, and the only other place I've seen it is at Little Italy in the city. Here we are looking out into the afternoon sun, watching sailboats lift along the breeze; we are beginning to relax and enjoy each other, and I'm glad I ordered the fried cheese.

"Mmm, this is good, share it with me, go ahead," she says, gesturing to the calamari, as she eats one of the four slices of mozzarella. As soon as she has room for words in her mouth, she resumes. "What does it look like? Okay, it's very steep, it's rough going, but it's worth it. There are bodies of water—a stream at the bottom of this chasm. You can get down there, but you have to be airlifted out."

"Why would you go down there then?"

"Because it's beautiful."

"Okay, good. How do you get to this claim?"

"By believing in yourself, by believing in me," she says.

I look at her. I want her to make up a myth about the long trail, the journey contained within a journey, the landmark of the triple-trunk tree, the lizard under red rock which sings directions. I sigh. I started this, but it's her claim. I dunk a piece of calamari in the aioli sauce, which is good, but could use a little more garlic.

She turns toward the bay, where a boat full of men is coming back from fishing. "They only do it to get loaded and kill something, don't you think?" I get the point about the men, but I wouldn't complain about spending the afternoon drinking beer and trailing string through water.

"Sure. But it is pretty out there. Let's rent a sailboat someday and go sailing—we could probably do it without killing anything," I say.

"I don't know how to sail."

"Neither do I."

"No way," she laughs at me.

"You're a good swimmer and the water's warm enough."

"There are sharks in the bay," she says.

So I give that up, though I still like the idea. "Let's go back to your claim if we can't go sailing. How would someone else get there, how would you describe the way to them?"

"They'd have to come up to the gate."

"There are gates?"

"Yes, gates and windows. First they'd have to look in the windows, so they'd know what was inside, and I could see who they were. I don't want anyone coming in under false pretenses. Mine or theirs."

"That's fair," I say. "All right, what do you intend to do with this claim?"

"Do?"

"Yeah, you know, are you planning to build dwellings, single or multiple family, make a development, a commune, farm, mine, fish, hunt, log…"

"I want to make my home there." She looks at me so seriously I wriggle in my chair, but I manage to return her look, follow it through. *Okay, make your home there, without me, behind the gates. But I've got the original claim document. I know how to use these things.* We eat quietly for a little bit. "I get a tax break if I make improvements on my house, right?" She changes the air.

"No, no tax breaks—you don't get taxed on this claim. Only on what you produce from it. The state may tax anything you mine or take from the ground or find a way to sell, but it can't tax the claim itself." I change my mind about using her claim form to barge in on the home she is making—too sneaky. I have as many sneaky thoughts as anyone, but I try to keep them out of my regular business. I have to figure out another way to let her know how I feel. "All right, we're almost done with the form. Any other distinguishing features on the land—waterfalls, for instance?"

"Oh, there's a waterfall. And there's a cave." She starts to talk about the cave and I get very dreamy, can barely hear her. Maybe it's the beer; I don't drink a lot anymore. "It's very beautiful inside the cave, there are holes in the walls, and when the wind comes through it makes music everywhere inside. It's special, not many women get to come there with me."

"How do you get there?" I'm trying hard not to hear Mary Martin singing, "It's not on any chart, you must find it with your heart..."

"You can't plan to go, you can't want to go, it happens when you're not thinking about it. You get there by letting go. I told you, it's not easy. You have to let go to get there."

An image of the first weekend we were lovers opens up for a moment. Toward the end of that weekend, four and a half years ago, she was spooning me, and I was trying to tell her, ashamed and scared, how much I wanted her to feed me one of the truffles we'd left on the night stand. She spoke into my ear, calmed me, reached into my body and knew me. It was all sensation, the hum of a tuning fork in her hands, as she pulled my belly up and held my whole face in her mouth. *Days of amber, nights of jade, you are the lover I would not trade for anything...* I turn from the memory to a sailboat that's directly in the path the sun makes on the water. It looks as if it might vanish into the shimmer if it stays there another minute.

"Look, there's a rainbow over there," she says.

It takes me a little while to see the rainbow over the Marin headlands. By now I know better than to read natural phenomena as omens. I go back to the last piece of mozzarella. It's very stringy —I catch a broad string of cheese on my tongue and pull it away from my hand. She stares at me. I enjoy her staring and my audacity. I curl the cheese around my tongue and finally snap the string.

"That's disgusting," she says, obviously pleased.

"I am not disgusting," but I am satisfied with the effect.

"I didn't mean to say you were disgusting—"

"I know you didn't." I try to wink at her, but I don't think she notices. I lick the cheese off my teeth. "One last thing, how do we know this claim is yours?"

That shocks her. "Because it's me."

"But we have some other claims filed for this same land."

"They can't own me, here I am, Sophie," and thumps her arms and chest. "This is my flesh and blood, you have to register it to me!"

I don't want to press it. "That seems good enough, ma'am, we'll seal it here and see what happens."

"Good," she says.

The rest of our dinner is served. I have something called Cajun chicken fettuccine, which she says looks like something I'd like, and I wince, unable to keep myself from wondering if I've made some terrible menu mistake before I remember she's glad when I order what I want, and she's never used appetite or taste to judge me. She has steamed clams. She likes to pull back the outer lips of the clam, expose its belly and the clit-like structure of its insides. "This is how you get the sand out of them," she says, dunking it in the broth, open that way.

"Uh huh," I say.

"I can't remember when I had a meal of steamed clams. This is wonderful." She opens another up like that, a big one, showing it to me. I stare at her, wondering if she's being seductive on purpose or out of habit. "Do you want it?"

It takes me too long to respond. "Yes," I say. She leans across the table and puts it in my mouth, but by the time it gets there, we've both decided it's easier to keep our past where it is. She can still feed me, and I can accept, but we hold the deeper hungers hostage in memory. Each of us has our reasons. I look down at my plate, and curl the last noodles around my fork.

We finish eating; she orders Irish coffee. I decide to say how I've been feeling. It takes me awhile. She recognizes my change in sentence structure, the way I start the sentence and then can't finish it, how I stop breathing. Because she knows this routine so well, I end it as quickly as I can. We both know I want to tell her; the longer I drag it out, the more nervous and impatient she gets, the more unhappy and frightened I am. I used to waste a lot of money on this anxious hedging when we talked by long-distance phone. Now it takes me about the length of this paragraph to get it out.

"Sophie," I say, "I know this is a terrible time for you, between moving and feeling forced to choose between Bendita and Marge. But I've been feeling bad about our relationship a little lately. I—I've been feeling like I take a lot of care of you, and you—"

I can't bring myself to say, "I want to be taken care of too. I deliberately stopped myself from bringing you flowers when you moved because it's been so long since you spontaneously brought me a present, any little thing. Still I want that, I want more attention, even if it hurts to expect it from you now."

Can't she see how edgy I've been? I want her not to shut me out even if she chooses to be alone, giving up Bendita and Marge. Or, if she chooses either or both of them, I want her to look at how I'm doing in the midst of her choices. This is a hard thing to confess.

I'm thirty-five, I live with my partner, whom I love. I'm supposed to be secure, I'm not all that jealous, and the pains between me and Sophie are mostly old pains. Yet when I'm on the bridge at night, commuting home after work, going over all these things in my mind, I don't understand where this maturity came from. How did I get to be the one who can always take care of herself, the one who knows it's impossible to require proof in loving? I don't want to be that strong.

Sophie raises one eyebrow. "C'mon, you can say it, Phil. What?"

"I guess I feel invisible to you, lately."

She looks away from me, away from the bay water, out into the dining room, up to the big fans studding the ceiling. Suddenly I realize I've engineered my own set-up, and hold my breath. She can't stop herself from what comes next, turning back to look me in the eyes. "I'm trying not to be defensive, I want to hear what you're saying. But it's hard not to have the same response—that I'm inadequate, that I can never give you what you want."

I keep forgetting this part of the pattern. Even though I can hear it coming three seconds before she says it, hearing it again makes me want to cry. I'll be damned if I'm going to cry in the middle of this ritzy restaurant, though. In fact, I'll be damned if I'll cry anywhere. But I figure since I've started, I might as well finish. "I'm not trying to say you're inadequate, I just don't feel like you're paying the attention you could be, that I want you to. You don't see how you affect me—your talk about splitting to Chicago, about not wanting to move into my neighborhood, about not feeling good about anybody. It's like when you gave me the keys to your house, and said 'I wouldn't have given these to you so soon except I wanted someone in the neighborhood to have them.'"

"Well, that was true, what should I have said?"

"You could have said—I'm giving these to you because I love you and trust you, and I really need you to respect my privacy right now."

"That would have been healthier," she nods.

We're both squirming, yet we're doing much better in this conversation than usual. Neither of us has thrown anything, resorted to name calling, or walked out.

"But I've been trying to be there for you. I tried to call you this week as soon as I knew you were unhappy, and I made this date to spend time with you as soon as I could."

Maybe I'm wrong, maybe it's my fear of being left out, or that other women are making fun of how much I care for Sophie, while she's off having a good time with someone else. And she's been different lately—considerate and thoughtful. When I was miserable, working late in the print shop Thursday night, I called to complain to her answering machine. She'd tried to call me right back, but the switchboard was closed. She said she'd made pop-corn and was trying to get me to watch TV with her after work, but she ended up eating the popcorn alone and going to sleep. I was comforted by that. Still, I'm not ready to let go of her I'm-never-enough-for-you lament.

"I still feel unseen. You know, I love you as much as Bendita or Marge do, and sometimes it doesn't seem like it matters to you."

"What is it about me," she says, mostly to herself, but I hear the frustration in her voice. We get quiet. We're full; the afternoon sun through the windows, the beer and Irish coffee, the closeness and the strain are making us both sad and tired. She pays with her credit card, and I give her cash for half. I resist the temptation to treat her—it's no time to try to engender gratitude.

"Let's walk a little bit," Sophie suggests. We start out along the seawall, the sailboat and yacht berths.

"I'm sorry," I say.

"Don't be sorry for saying what you feel. I'm just afraid you think I'm someone that I'm not, that you keep waiting for me to be who you want me to be."

I start to argue, but then reconsider. "Maybe I do." I kick at a stone in the path. The harbor, the sky, turn a dull granite, as if we had entered a black and white movie. "I try to see who you are, I keep trying to see you honestly. But I—" She makes a motion as if to take my arm, to start to hold me, or to touch me, and then withdraws it. I'm glad she doesn't touch me then, and glad she had the impulse. We change the subject; I let color drain slowly back into the world.

We talk about ambition and class, how you get things and how you want them—a boat, for instance. What her mother did to her, how she doesn't understand how to get from an idea to reality. She has lots of ideas. I start to give her the pep talk about how she can do what she wants if she would only choose something and go for it. How she has resources she doesn't even know about, inside and outside.

"Like what?" she asks.

"Like creativity, and—"

"Oh, never mind, honey, we've been here before. Talking about how much wood I could chuck if I only chose to chuck wood."

"No, I suppose not. Beautiful boats, though."

"Aren't they? I'd love to have a boat some day."

"Me too. Remember when we were going to own a houseboat together?"

"You wanted me to own it so you could come play on it," Sophie punches me softly on the arm, an easier form of touch to share.

I'm smiling. "No, we were going to own it together."

"Don't you remember we were looking at them when I visited you in Oregon and you said I should buy you one?"

"Oh yeah—but then later I said we should own one together, as an experiment, but we bought the Trivial Pursuit game together instead."

"Oh, that's why we did that. Well, I don't mind owning Trivial Pursuit with you." She rubs my arm with her hand for a second. We are standing at the end of the concrete, staring out at the boats.

"Maybe I shouldn't have said anything," I say.

"Honey, knock it off. It's time to head back. My feet hurt in these shoes. "

I sleep in Sophie's new house for the first time that night. First I rub her neck and shoulders for an hour while we watch TV, she beats me twice at cribbage, and then she bakes packaged apple turnovers for a late dessert, which we eat while watching a simulated log burn in the fireplace. I haven't planned to spend the night, but Bendita is sick and left a message canceling her date with Sophie, and my partner is visiting her mother in the Southwest.

"Do you want me to drive you home?" She's already in her nightshirt.

"Would you like me to stay?"

"If you want to."

"I'd like to if you want me to."

"Fine."

I make a face at her and she throws a couch pillow at me. "I need something to sleep in."

"Oh yeah, this is the first time you've slept here, isn't it?" She finds an old T-shirt of mine in her dresser.

I restrain myself from making too much of either of those things—the off-handed invite, the intimacy of clothing that nestles in my ex-lover's drawer.

"Is this my toothbrush?"

"Yes," she says, and doesn't add that I had badgered her about remembering to move it. We're doing our best to behave.

She falls asleep beside me while I read. Later, in the dark, I can hear the creek running beside the window, and match my breath to the rhythm of water over rock. The warmth and harbor of her body come to me without the old bright desire. I grieve for that desire even as I welcome this unfamiliar calm.

In the morning, she's quick to invite me naked into the shower, but as the spray plasters her dark hair flat on her head and she experiences my drawing near, she looks up in surprise. I suspect many of her invitations surprise her. Her invitation to feed me clams, her invitation to bathe. She might say she only wants to be close, to be easy. I accept because I want closeness, keep looking to extend the tenderness, but I know to remain on guard.

We soap each other a little, grazing bellies as we share the hot water, admiring each other's size secretly, feeling both proud and guilty for breaking the rules which define beauty. When we talk about being fat, usually we bitch about how hard it is in the world. But we have times when it's fine. Even if we can't be delicious to each other now, we can share this unnameable, outlaw pleasure. Maybe that's why she likes to shower with me. I stare at my wet toes, considering it, long after she's gotten out to dry.

"Should I make us some breakfast?" Sophie calls from the kitchen.

"Sure, I love to have femmes cook for me."

"You are so—" I can tell she's narrowing her eyes, and I'm glad to miss that.

"Don't worry," I yell back, "I'll do the dishes."

Later, when I have my hands in the dishwater, she's looking for her car keys.

"You know," I say, "I never really understand why you broke up with me."

Sophie swivels. "But I'm still here," she says.

HOUSES

I had been away for awhile. I was lying beside her. I was lying on her. It was morning, and my head was on her breast. We were sleepy and beginning to be aware of each other. I closed my eyes and had an image of a front porch somewhere, with two screen doors, behind which the house doors were open. Looking in, the house was dark.

"I'm thinking of you as if you were a house," I said, reaching across her belly, opening my eyes.

"What kind of a house?" she asked.

"A big house, with lots of rooms, and downstairs a kind of scary unfinished basement. But upstairs, rooms filled with light."

"Like a house on a Southern street," she said.

"More like an old house in a small New England town in the fall," I said. She moved her body the small amount closer it could get to me, flesh lapping into flesh. "The kind of house where a woman, thinking herself alone at night, pushes her head against a yellow kitchen wall and weeps. Then the next day, at dusk, the woman sits on the porch of you on an old wooden bench, feeling a contentment she never thought she would get to."

She said, "If I were a house, I would give you the key."

MY GRANDMOTHER'S PLATES

Fifteen years after my grandmother died, my Aunt Glory sends me a box containing my grandmother's glass plates and matching goblets. A note precedes them: "Your mother and I thought you should have something material that belonged to Rose. I have used them for years—they're a very handy size for salads and lunch."

A week later, I am carrying the box home from the post office. I set it on the couch and hold my breath. I remember the carpet in my grandmother's dining room, the newspapers over the carpet, the heavy wood sideboards, a needlepoint replica of the unicorn tapestries that one of my grandmother's sisters made. I loved my grandmother, and she loved me. I was never very attached to the rest of my family. After Grandma Rose died, I moved farther north, then far west.

My grandmother kept kosher on the eighth floor of West End and 86th Street in New York City. I had a key. When she traveled, visiting her daughters, I'd bring my high school friends in to smoke dope, make love, sit naked on her furniture—but I never let them touch the dishes. I only let them eat take-out on paper plates. "Grandma," I'd say, "don't worry, you can trust me, I never mix the meat and milk, I never let anyone into the cupboards."

Now I open the box not knowing what to expect. A heavy, square goblet appears, alternating panels and circles of clear and rose. The plate matches. *Yes,* I think, *a handy size, a little bigger than salad but not a full dinner plate.* I can only take out one glass, one dish. I leave them there, on the couch. Do I recognize them, are they ghosts? "Don't bother to thank me," my aunt wrote, "I know how busy you are, that's why I got a return receipt." Although I have been trained to behave better, I take her permission and don't send a note.

Fifteen years after my grandmother's death I'm thirty-nine—why did they decide to send these to me now? After finally visiting my home, did they decide I was too poor, would never have wedding presents? Or did I become real somehow, and they have decided to reconnect me to them, to tradition? Are these meat or milk dishes? Were they used every day or only for Pesach? I think I remember them, but when I close my eyes to visualize, I see the box of crackers in the oven, the tiny kitchen, the matzo meal in the closet above the ironing board, and my throat closes around the smell of chicken soup in the hallway.

My aunt, who keeps kosher still, sent these between Purim and Pesach. Maybe it was spring cleaning, and she held a feather in her mind—some *chumetz*[1] in a corner—something she thought she owed me or something of her own that needed new space—*clear these out, send them away.* I question my mother in the mail, and her answer is sweet, but the same: "We were thinking you didn't have anything from your grandmother, and we wanted you to have these."

I have grandmother's menorah, and a few little things I took when she died. But those are what I took, not what they gave. Maybe they both feel guilty that I didn't get the writing desk I'd asked for; or maybe it's the way women express their fear of mortality—handing down their rings, their plates. *We will be all*

---

[1] *Leavened food. Just before Passover, orthodox Jewish women clean their houses thoroughly, after which there's a ritual where the house is swept with a feather to get any stray crumbs of chumetz that may linger and spoil the kosherness of Passover, when only unleavened food may be eaten.*

right, everything will go well with us if you don't break the dishes, if you carry them with you when you move, if you send them to your nieces when you have some—unbroken dishes down three generations means extraordinary luck, for Jews, no pogroms, no forced evacuations.

I keep the open box full of dishes on my couch for two weeks until I have a lesbian meeting in the house and have to move it to the back porch. I feel I cannot use them until I've koshered them somehow, changed them from kosher to mine. Performed some ritual that keeps faith with the faith of the women who've gone before me. Something instinctual, female, that has nothing to do with intellectual belief.

How do you kosher dishes? I ask my friends. They say you take them to the ocean and dip them in salt water. Ocean water koshers objects. Of course this ritual has been modified to salt water in the kitchen and a couple of prayers, since Jews in the Diaspora are often far from the sea. Or, they say, "You could take them to a mikve." I'm not sure this is true, but I develop an elaborate fantasy of carrying these glass plates into the San Francisco mikve.

I've never been to a mikve, I don't know if my mother has ever been to a mikve, certainly she's never spoken about one. A mikve is a ritual bath, where women go after menstruating, to make themselves "clean" again. I've seen one in the Jewish movies, something about being immersed in the water, a dunking and turning.

In my mind the mikve is in an ancient cave, tile protruding from limestone ledges, fed by an underground passage to the sea, heated dangerously, mysteriously. I imagine small groups of orthodox women dropping their towels, letting their real hair fall around their necks, stepping carefully down the slippery limestone steps.

Into this steamy yellow cave I carry my brown box full of clear and rose glass plates. I put the box on the side of the pool and first immerse myself in whatever ritual is given me by the woman attending the bath, making sure every hair on my head has been submerged in the metallic-tasting water. Bobbing up, naked, I pull the dishes and goblets out one by one, dunk them in the mikve, wrap them in clean towels, place them back in the box while the orthodox women watch, smiling at me.

The dishes stay on my back porch. Eventually I write my aunt a thank you note. I don't lug them to the Pacific, I don't find the mikve. Every now and then I think about it, tripping on the box while opening or closing the back porch window. Lag b'Omer, Shavous, Tish b'Av, all the minor Jewish holidays, go by without notice.

Then, on the second day of Rosh Hashanah, I invite my friend Sophie over for breakfast—bagels, whitefish salad, lox, avocado, onion, tomato, cream cheese. I go to the cupboard to get plates and stop still. "Oh," I say, "it's the new year; I know just what we'll use."

Two plates come out of the box. It's that simple. Sophie, who's my neighbor and dear friend, listens to my story about the plates and the mikve, but concentrates on the lox. We enjoy our new year's feast.

The plates—seem very pretty. Almost too pretty to be mine. Two plates in the dish drainer, in the stack in the cupboard. All the others, and the goblets, wait on the porch. I am very careful with these two dishes, I only eat fish and dairy on them, never meat.

I used to say my family never gave me anything, not anything from the heart.

MY GRANDMOTHER PLAY

<u>Characters</u>

Phyllis—a lesbian in her late forties, early fifties, dressed in jeans, a casual shirt, tennis shoes.

Deborah—her mother, of an indeterminate age over 70, in a print dress and costume jewelry—long beads, long earrings. "Well put together" but not showy.

<u>Stage setting</u>

A home office—along one side a large old wooden desk, a computer set up, many paper files, some in a vertical holder. A rolling office chair. Along the back wall sits a long table covered with stacks and stacks of paper. Beside the table, a filing cabinet and a battered wooden army footlocker. A large round clock above the table has the wrong time on it. A bookcase or two would be appropriate.

As the stage lights go up, the woman enters from the side opposite the desk. She sits down, turns on the computer, stands up, shuffles some papers on the table. Looks over her shoulder at the audience.

Phyllis: In almost every stack of these (gestures to the papers), somewhere there's a reference to how my grandmother died.

(She goes to the desk, sits, picks up a page.) This was from a novel I started twenty-five years ago. (Reads page) "Her grandmother gets in, who begs and begs for her turn, wrapping in ribbons against the time: speak my eyes and my burnt hands. Next. That's next." (Puts the paper down)

Fifteen versions. (She gestures to the computer.) Maybe not that many. Two or three full tries, and allusions in a handful of other stories.

(Stands.) Here's the deal. I was twenty-three years old. One night, in the middle of a meeting of my collective household of the time, I got a call from my mother—wait. I don't actually remember who called. My mother or my brother. "There's been an accident. Grandma's in the hospital."

She was eighty-four or eighty-two. She lived alone in an apartment in New York City, on the corner of West End Ave and 86th Street, a neighborhood where many Jewish and white grand-mothers lived in the 1970's. She liked living there. "I can walk to everything, Sloans grocery store—at the corner. Schraffts—down the block." When I was a child, she took me on those errands with her, reintroducing me every year to the man in the bookstore/card shop where she picked up paperback mysteries, letting me stare at the cases of foreign cigarettes with French and Arabic labels at the tobacconist.

My grandmother smoked two packs, maybe three, of unfil-tered Chesterfields every day of her life, starting when she was young, sometime before women got the vote, and it was a daring, modern thing for a young woman to do. She told me once that she'd marched in a suffrage parade down Fifth Avenue.

(Phyllis sits down in the chair, spins around, sticks her legs out at the audience, then leans forward.) When you're a kid, a teenager, everything that happened before you were born—doesn't matter when. Alexander the Great, the Pyramids of Egypt, the conversion of the Hindu King Asoka to Buddhism, the suffrage movement—they all happened at more or less the same time. A long time ago. Because you have the right to vote, and your mother has it, it's hard to conceive of how recently it was won. "Am I right?" That's what my grandmother always said, "Am I right?"

So when your grandmother tells you she marched for suffrage, before women had the vote, it's a kick in the head. I mean, I was proud of her, hey, my grandma, she was hip, she was an activist! But jeez, for the vote? It's that peculiar moment when history gets up close to you and breathes in your face with its garlic breath, its rotting teeth.

(A soft knock. She looks at the door. A soft knock again.)

I think my mother would like to get a word in here—

(Deborah walks in, slowly. She has a bright print dress on, a long strand of beads. She holds a cigarette, unlit.)

Deborah: She was eighty two. And I would have hardly called Mother an activist. (She exits, the same direction she came in.)

Phyllis: (Calling after Deborah) What did I know about perspective? I only had Grandma's word for it. Where was I? (Gets up, peers out the "door" her mother came and left by.)

One of them called, and I made arrangements to get down to New York City that night. The collective was a few miles north of Amherst, Massachusetts. Some professor someone knew was driving to Brooklyn. I called my mother to let her know. She was in my grandmother's apartment.

(Deborah comes in, stands by the door, appearing much younger this time. She and Phyllis mime a telephone conversation.)

Deborah: But you'll get in so late. You don't know how grueling it's been. I don't want you to wake me. Take a bus tomorrow.

Phyllis: But I have a ride picking me up in half an hour. Don't worry, Mom, I'll stay with Steve in his dorm.

Deborah: You will not wake your brother up.

Phyllis: But Mom, he's a college student, I stay with him all the time.

Deborah: You will not wake your brother up at two in the morning.

Phyllis: Don't worry about me! (Slams the phone down, throws it across the room. Deborah keeps standing by the door, no light on her.)

Pshew! I scared the women in the collective, but it wasn't the first time I'd thrown something. (Reflective) Don't do that anymore. Not often. Anyway. I'd been reading Jill Johnston, that tells you how long ago it was. I think it was Johnston who coined the phrase "lesbian nation"—she wrote a book with that title, as I recall. She used to have a column in *The Village Voice,* and she'd recently written a psychological rumination about how the mothers will always choose the sons. I spent the whole trip to New York in a rage because my mother chose my brother over me, his sleep and comfort, not mine, in this crisis. Like it was him who was supposed to be there, and I could come later. I was the extra, not the one she needed.

Deborah: I—

Phyllis: You're still here?

Deborah: I don't think that's what was going through my mind then. I'm not sure that's fair. And I thought we'd made up.

Phyllis: We have. But I'm not sure my analysis is wrong, either. Not even now.

Deborah: It was such a terrible time. (Leaves)

Phyllis: (Looking after her) It was. (Turning back to audience) I had a friend who lived in Brooklyn—or maybe I stayed on a couch in the place where the professor was going. In the morning when I went out on the street, everyone had a little smudge of ash on their forehead. One of those things you can't make up. It must have been a Catholic neighborhood, a Puerto Rican neighborhood. It was Ash Wednesday.

(A projection on the wall, or even a real group of people walking through, with ashes on their foreheads, wearing street clothes and business suits.)

(Phyllis is silent for a minute, sits in the chair, swivels, looks down at her hands.) The next thing I remember is being in the hospital, outside of ICU. (Looks up)

Intensive care unit. Just because we live in alphabet soup doesn't necessarily mean you know the initials. Of course most of you have gone through death, haven't you? You can't get past forty without your grandparents, your parents, maybe a lover or friend with AIDS, with breast cancer, heart attack, stroke, car accident, drive by shooting. One of my friends knows two lesbians who were murdered. Murdered.

I often get the image of sea turtles hatching—all those little flipper-footed babies poking up from the sand, making their instinctive dash for the sea, while the birds circle and dive, trying to eat them. That's us—sea turtles dashing for the sea. Maybe Darwin was wrong—the fittest don't necessarily survive. Even the fittest, the fastest, the least hesitant, the one closest to the wave can be caught in the cross hairs of a diving predator.

(Deborah pokes her head in, gives a look.)

Okay, I'm getting to it. (Stands up.)

My mother, my brother, my aunt and her husband were conferring with the doctor. Friend of the family doctor—my parents and he and his wife had adjacent apartments, matching infants, right after the war. World War Two. So Grandma was getting good care.

I didn't tell you what happened?

Oh right—(She sits back down and looks at the computer, presses a couple page up buttons. The first row might see text passing on the screen.) history, garlic breath, suffrage. Two packs of Chesterfields. (Turns from the computer.)

It was night. She had on a nightgown. She was walking in the hall and a hot ash from her cigarette fell on the nightgown. It went up like a torch.

They said she had the presence of mind to roll in the bathtub and put the fire out, put on a clean nightgown before the firemen came.

She had third degree burns on most of her body.

(Slaps one hand against the other, looks away) That's what happened to her.

I only remember fragments of what the adults were talking about outside the ICU. I was twenty-three, I told you that? So my brother was about twenty. Finally they decided us kids could go in, though I could tell they didn't really want to let us. They made us as sterile as they could—masks, gowns, gloves.

It was a theory they had then—maybe they still have it—to expose a burn victim totally to air to let her heal.

This was during the Vietnam War. We used to see photographs on the nightly news of napalmed children, people running, burning.

But when you see it—in the flesh—with hospital disinfectant not covering up but compounding that burnt smell—

Well. I looked in my grandmother's eyes. I never saw anyone's eyes look like that, never heard anyone describe it. Her eyes had a gray film over them, and at the same time were clear, staring out beyond herself into death. She reached for my hand. I held it very lightly in the glove.

"It's me, Grandma."

"Cold," my grandmother said. Then she shifted behind her eyes, and tried to recognize me. "Go to the corner, to Sloans, and get me six oranges."

(She wipes tears from her eyes)

I'm sorry. (Pause) It's what? Twenty-six, thirty years later—
(She has to stop, get up, shake off the thing that overwhelms her
before she goes on.)

"Cold," she said. She was trembling from cold and shock.

I thought to distract her; I told her my first novel was going
to get published. It wasn't, you know, that I cared about that
right then, it was—she was always so proud of me, she kept every
school newspaper I ever had a column in, in a drawer in the
wooden breakfront by the chair she always sat in.

I wanted to put another thought in her mind, bring her close
to me. She stuttered. "Pub -publi - that's good. Get the oranges
from Sloans."

She was looking at me like a wild beast, her tiny body sav-
aged, torn to shreds. If I agreed that we were standing in her hallway, under the mica star lamp, if I agreed with her that this could
be a normal visit, that I was her good girl, going to do an errand,
then—I could see it underneath the film on her eyes—oh god!

(She's crying freely now, though still trying not to, wiping
the tears from under her glasses, pulling her glasses off to wipe
her face. Goes to the desk to get a tissue to blow her nose. Takes
a breath.)

If I agreed, then we wouldn't be in the ICU, she wouldn't be
lying naked in front of my brother and me, all the nurses, this
wouldn't have happened, we could go back—

"Yes, grandma, I'll get the oranges."

I looked at my brother. He shook his head. I looked at the
clock (She looks up at her wall clock.)—I was going to put a new
battery in that, and then I thought, why bother? I have a watch.
The old battery must have a little juice still because it's a different
time every time I come down here. (Takes a breath.)

The nurse said we had to leave.

That was the last time I saw my grandmother alive, though I didn't know it would be. This part in the middle is hazy—she lived a week. A week like that. They knew she couldn't live long—something about the kidneys processing fluid, skin grafts—even if she healed from the burns. She was eighty-four. I think her doctor, my mother, my aunt, me—we would have all agreed to let her go. Oh, maybe I'm wrong. You know. (Starts to cry again.) There's something in Jewish law about suffering, about not letting animals suffer. But it's so hard when you can't believe—when you want—when you think your will can change a tragedy back—

She lived a week. I went home for a couple days. I had a job or a class or—I don't know what. I remember now, my leg had been broken, I was a week or two out of the cast. Limping around. I stayed that night with my mother in my grandmother's apartment? Or I went right back?

(She looks at the door.)

Mom? (No response.)

Well, anyway, when I came back to New York I went right to the hospital. I sat outside the ICU for an hour, and no one was there. No answer at the phone in the apartment. Finally a nurse came over. "No one told you?" I looked inside—the bed had been stripped.

I took the cross-town bus to my grandmother's apartment. I had the keys. I think I still have them—(She gestures to the footlocker.)—in there—and the piece of black cloth they give you—because it's traditional to tear your clothes, but no one wants to tear their clothes, or see anyone else do it.

(She stands up, tugs at her shirt as if to rip it, kind of laughs.) It's not easy to do, either. So they give you this black scrap of fabric, already torn, and you pin it to your clothes.

My grandmother was orthodox. So the funeral service—the women sat on one side, the men on the other. I sat next to my mother. I thought: *now she has to rely on me.*

(Deborah re-enters, wearing a plain dark coat to which a ribbon of black cloth is pinned. She takes a few steps toward Phyllis.)

Deborah: But I've always relied on you. You were just so far away. (She reaches out, the woman takes her arm, escorts her back to the side of the stage where she stands by a pile of dirt. The woman moves front center). My brother, passing by me as we filed out, whispered, "We'll have our day." What a weak response, I remember thinking. What are we gonna do, wait around for the whole generation to croak? And at that exact moment, when the patriarchy had thrown me where I wanted to be. I don't remember saying anything to him.

I'd never been at a burial before. I think I went to the funeral of one of my grandmother's brothers, but it's a way distant memory. That afternoon lots of cars, maybe three or four small Cadillac limousines, wound their way to the cemetery—in Queens.

Deborah: Don't leave out how the hearse passed Mother's shul, and the men came out and said a blessing. It was a big honor because they didn't do that for women. She wouldn't want you to leave that out.

Phyllis: Thank you. No, she wouldn't. (To the audience) And I would have left it out.

So. We were at the grave. (She moves to the pile of dirt, standing opposite her mother.) Plain pine casket, lowered into the ground. Something about that—when the casket goes in the grave—(She chokes back tears). You have to let it go. And you can't. When someone is a part of you, all these tiny fibers (She rubs her chest, her arms)—did you ever study one-celled organisms, how they have these tiny hairs that they use to propel themselves or have sex? It's like that—we have all these fine invisible threads coming out of us, and they attach to the web of the people we belong with. This is not a new idea. My threads to my grandmother were very strong.

Deborah: You were her favorite grandchild. Everyone knew it.

Phyllis: Thanks. (To the audience) But favorite—that doesn't matter. She was dead. What counted was what I felt for her.

You know, her apartment was the only place that stayed the same throughout my life until then. My story with my parents—it's too complicated for right now (Mother and Woman look at each other). My story with my grandmother was relatively uncomplicated, even when I was a teenager and used to think, *come the revolution, grandma, you'll have to go*—on account of her pride in her coat from Saks Fifth Avenue, and how furious she was when I went to see "Marat/Sade" in my jeans. Didn't stop me from buying flowers for her. At the corner, in front of Sloans.

Anyway. What I didn't know about funerals was that you were supposed to throw a symbolic shovel full of dirt into the grave. Good idea, really. But I was shocked at first, watching. My mother and her sisters went first.

(Deborah steps closer to the grave.)

Deborah: (Crying, miming throwing shovel after shovel in) Poor little mother. Poor little mother.

Phyllis: For the first time, my mother looked bent and old to me. (She looks at Deborah, who rests the shovel, looks back. Phyllis sighs) Oh, Mom—. (Deborah passes the shovel.)

Then it was my turn. This was March. International Women's Day, actually.

Deborah: Mother was always afraid she'd die in the winter, and the ground would be so frozen the grave diggers wouldn't be able to dig.

Phyllis: I took a shovel full off the mound beside the grave, and threw it down. You can hear a little echo from the coffin, the pebbles bouncing around. It's a good ritual, really. It allows you to be in pain at the same time that it makes you move, pushes you to act. It's you who does this thing. (Turns to Deborah) You bury your mother. (Deborah nods, Phyllis turns away) Your grandmother. So you know she's gone.

After that—I stayed with my mother in the apartment while we sat shiva. Jews sit for a week—not sitting all the time, of course. Mostly moving around, fidgeting. Sending the kids to the deli for more lox. Adjusting the black cloths that drape the mirrors, because you're not supposed to be concerned with your own image or personal vanity, for seven days. Also a superstition about spirits, how they get trapped, trying to reenter through the mirror. (Pauses.) And you're supposed to sit on little boxes, I guess the idea is to eschew worldly comfort. The funeral home sends over little cardboard stools—I think they were only supposed to be symbolic, or maybe to have extra seating, because the house is crowded. One of my mother's sisters stays in a hotel, the other lives nearby.

My mother sleeps in my grandmother's bed—wait—I was sleeping by the window? (Looks at Deborah.)

Deborah: I had been there all that time. I couldn't sleep in her bed.

Phyllis: (To Deborah) It's okay, Mom. (They embrace, then step back.)

I slept in my grandmother's bed. I woke up and saw that ash had settled on my arm.

Deborah: Her nightgown.

Phyllis: Her flesh.

(Lights dim. Deborah takes a step back. Phyllis goes to desk, picks up a piece of paper, puts it down.)

Phyllis: So... I started to dream about my grandmother's apartment. First they had saved it for me, exactly as it was. Then the furniture started to get moved out, piece by piece. Sometimes I'm down in the street and can't get up. Sometimes I'm in the back hallway without a key. Once I knocked on the door and another woman was living there, but she let me in. I showed her how everything had been arranged.

I still have this dream, not so frequently, or at least, not that I'm aware of. But this week I dream I'm sitting on her radiator, looking down on 86th street. She comes in from the hallway. I'm surprised, delighted. "You're still alive!"

Deborah: (From the shadows) "What else should I be," she says.

Curtain

SLIDING

Coefficient of sliding friction: the ratio of the force it takes to get two surfaces to slide on one another when they're at rest.

They had been resting. One on another. Acquaintances peered at their lives through tiny peepholes slit in the mass of ribbons with which they surrounded themselves. The way the viewers squinted, shifting from foot to foot, the ribbons whapping their faces, gave the sensation of movement. Everyone said they were moving—elaborating on descriptions of dramatic scenes, of events that gave dimension to communal history, of adventures and exploits that became the romantic literature of their generation.

But they were not moving like that. They were still resting. They were not given to squint back or savor the motion of others outside their ribbon-fitted parlor, which was one of the reasons so many took the opportunity to peek in.

The same music played on the radio. They played the same game of cards. They had the same argument. They had the same win/loss ratio. They had the same meal and they thanked each other the same way, went to bed the same number of nights and turned the same directions in their sleep.

They loved each other in this way, at rest, if not at ease, for a long time. They had the same bitterness out of which they wove the tiny hammocks where their memories slept. The hammocks and the memories moved so gently in the ribboned wind, it was hard to remember where the bitterness came in.

The meals they cooked were not spectacular, but they were delicious and abundant. They took the same pleasure in eating persimmons and had the same fury about the damage done to their bodies, hearts and sex, which they went over in the same way before turning out the light. Limestone dust collected in the folds of their skin, blown west from fossil reefs beyond the high desert.

Occasionally one read to the other, the same story.

What does it take to get them sliding? Not simply lubrication, nor yet the smooth confluence of surface—on both counts they had plenty. We've all seen pictures of the batter gliding into base, slick rubber on dirt slipping in. The two of them turned their heads and sighed. If there is a pitch, they are not seduced into taking a swing.

But eventually every equation has its outsider—she who walks through the curtain, doesn't know the rules of the game, brings a new hunger, a different schedule, a taste for slippery motion. A woman who won't blink, who wants all the angles, who challenges the values. The coefficient.

Then the sliding begins.

THE BOTTOM

There's a tunnel that ends at solid rock. It's dark. It's always dark in there. People dream of this tunnel all the time.

Some say it means sex, some say fear, some say death, some say tunnel, tunnel, tunnel and to hell with you symbolists.

One year, in December, we were hiking, both sick. I had stopped wearing the eye patch a week before, but my muscles were still stiff and twitching, and I had a cold. She'd been rear-ended, may still have been wearing a neck brace. My feet were bad, and I was using a cane. Nevertheless: Pinnacles national monument, the middle of California. We had a certain kind of mid-thirties dyke pride in taking up a challenge. And of course, the desire to hold intimacy through the waning of desire (nothing can damage us enough to keep us from the cornucopia). We'd come that far.

The path is beautiful—green in strips running between round red boulders, rocky pools wearing collars of late wildflower, some kind of white seed pod thick in places on the ground.

We have flashlights, for the cave. First the trail leads into a narrow corridor, funneling through stone until we think it is the tunnel, so we turn the flashlights on. Water drips down the wall, water is always dripping down the wall in stories about tunnels and caves.

Because it does. Caves are mostly wet places. We think wet dark places are sex but maybe they're only caves. It's hard to tell geography from biology. I was always such a good student that it's strange now to be mixing up the subjects.

Are dreams psychology or literature? Is memory physiology or the history of film? Is this the advanced course?

"This cave isn't so impressive," she says. She kisses me before we leave the tunnel and bump into sunlight. Before I can say it she does, poking fun at me. "You always want to kiss me in beautiful places."

But this is not exactly lust's good season, so I turn to jab my cane at the trail ahead, scouring boulders with the good eye. Suddenly it isn't clear which way to go. Not well marked. We scout up, down, around a rocky slope, not wanting to go back. She has a goat nature and can scramble up and down better than I, even recently injured. I have a good, slow sense of orientation, of which way is next.

Between us we find a descent. Should we really be going in here? A hole, and no light showing. Slippery, hard, too dark, unmarked. The park service couldn't mean this—it's too obscure. The park service is not supposed to let you do anything dangerous, is it? The park service is not allowed to scare you. We pay taxes for clear signs, for trail guides.

But down we swagger. The flashlight bounces off walls, all of them gray, thick, hard; I dislodge a trickling avalanche of pebbles. Too quickly we are in deep. I don't know if I can climb up the way we've come down. I let the flashlight lick up the incline for a minute, and then I know I can't climb back. Maybe she could. Maybe she could go for help. Stop. We don't need help, do we? Not us. But then we hear how our breath catches in our throats. What else is down here, in the cave?

Insect, animal, skeleton, gas, the souls of trapped miners, journey to the center of the Earth, snakes, monsters? They poke our soft ribs, snicker in our hair. *Who told you to come here? Who said you could?*

Look for water. I told you, there is always water in this story. Follow where it goes. The ground has a long stain in a deep streak below our feet. I pull the light along the string of water, clenching my jaw. Someone panicked in a labyrinth, I remember, but it's not going to be me. My lover breathes shallowly, and her cheeks have gone cold, which I know although I am not touching her and her stiff back is in front of me.

As the beam follows the water, it finds daylight in a crack forty, sixty, two hundred feet from where we slid down. Hard to measure distance when you're scared. "There," she says—and we transport ourselves across the dark, pressing out into another green canyon bottom, surprised and delighted with ourselves, the trail beneath us clear again.

"That wasn't so bad, was it?" She grimaces like someone trying not to look embarrassed.

"No," I say, filling with regret that I'd been so frightened, that I hadn't spent another ten minutes, another hour, pressing my palms, my breasts against the walls, turning the flashlight out, finding something beyond fear to run my hands on in the cave. Holding my lover's body, rubbing the bones of her neck in the dark, listening to the peculiar flutter of our organs stretched to sense our selves again. If you let anxiety awaken you until you stop trembling, can recognition come back in? Could I have found her again? Would she have known me there?

We amble on, companionable and quiet, both in our memories of being in a bottom we did not recognize until we left. The trail back is much longer and steeper than we expect, and we meet no one except a young woman, the park ranger. She says, "Yes, it wouldn't be any fun if they'd marked the cave too clearly, would it?"

GRACE

Grace looks at me, her dark jade eyes big and glittering. "Where did you find those stockings?"

She moves like fog, propels herself in a sharp gust toward my outstretched arm, where the stockings drape over the muscle and tick against my naked belly.

She—comes over me—a weather, a mood, an impulse.

"Oh, they *are* silk!" She rubs the long seam against her soft chin. Grace believes the chin is a true tactile gauge, an instrument overlooked by dykes who only count on their fingers. "Fingers are all right when you have to change a light bulb, or... you know..." (*I* knew.) "But for fine sentiment, rub a girl's arm with your chin, maneuver so you can get your chin against her inner thigh. It's the delicate things we do that really matter, isn't it?"

I try to always agree with Grace; most of the time it's easy, like saying thank you when you're offered a piece of lemon meringue pie. Now Grace's chin approves the stockings, the fine hard line of the seam, the oyster fresh feel of black silk, the gift of them, the surprise offering.

Me, I live by deadlines, I know how long everything takes, I make allowances for flat tires on the bridge, I arrive nine times out of ten exactly two minutes ahead of time. I enjoy structure; it makes me feel free to play in the open space between limits. My lover may take two hours to come and, knowing it, I lie back and bask in the hours as they go by. I make sure to have enough time, and I have a contingency plan in case time runs out. Time is always running out—it skitters sideways out the door, taking on the body of a ten year old girl who can't bear her homework another minute longer, who has to get on her bicycle and peddle or burst. I'm the one who knows all that, who manages it, watches, counts, schedules, knows what to do with every spare moment, can make a plan to have fun from 9 to 11:45 and stick to it.

Grace, of course, could care less. It gets done or doesn't, she weaves herself into time the way I hope she'll weave herself into these stockings. Every moment's a luxury, and if the luxury is strong and clear, she'll forget her lunch date as easily as the book review she's supposed to mail tomorrow. She'll move into the silk and stroke my neck with her warm soft chin, and her breath will smell of lemon and cinnamon. Her skin sliding into silk, her hands silk, her dark eyes slide, everything is silk all around me, and me, I have enough time for it now, however long it lasts.

WHAT LOVE IS

Everyone asks for love stories. Solicitations in the mail, on the computer, from friends. What do they expect? Patent intimacy, encouragement, vindication? You used to get away with telling adventure stories—the lesbian separatist Fourth of July canoe disaster, the time an alligator nearly chomped you in the Everglades, or how dyke patrol trashed an abusive man's car at 3 a.m., spray-painting "rapist" all over it, parked in front of his suburban ranch house. You used to say romantic love was a heterosexual plot, created to drive women to distraction and submission. Remember that?

Now you're over fifty, distracted and—submissive? Cultures swing back and forth, everyone knows that. Smart folks get out of the way of the pendulum before they get clocked. Okay, so it's not funny. But clocked and plot have an off-rhyme that ties the first two paragraphs together. Writers think about these things, even if they rarely talk about it. Today you want to expose the gears, the mechanisms, underlying pattern. And you can tell love stories, if that's what fashion dictates. You don't mean to brag, but you actually know what love is.

You look at the way women's cheeks turn red in the sunlight, the way the old women in the public pool shield themselves from the sun while the young ones splash in whatever covers their nipples and pubic bones. You notice two Chinese American girls—they look like girls to you, but maybe they're twenty—who introduced themselves at the beginning of the week, now coming hand in hand, splashing through the slow lane with kick boards and flippers, talking. One of them shows off long sleek black hair, the other's is cropped, dyed orange. In the pool shower, you offer soap to the old woman who wears a straw hat and leotards under her bathing suit. All this is love—the quotidian love you get used to in yourself, the kind that makes life tolerable.

Once, driving through the redwoods, you stopped at a popular tree. Americans choose trees the same way they choose prom queens—by their awesome measurements. If you're going to look at any of them at all, make sure to check this one out. You used to drive through the redwoods often, because you lived in Oregon for five years and had a long distance lover in Oakland for two of them. Sometimes love is a good excuse for a ride. It's eight or nine hours from the southern Oregon coast, where you lived, to the Bay, and those hours, driving with your dog, singing show music as the road dipped out of forest to cup the ocean in its asphalt hands, were a meditational ecstasy. Simple, singular truths would shrug off the great redwood branches with the morning mist; joy would flop along into the mouth of a pelican scooping up dinner; bitterness would be ameliorated on the ride home by reaching into the lunch your lover packed and finding a purple sequined star.

You stopped at most of the short trails and wayside nature attractions at least once. At the most popular tree, it was easy to notice how many hiking boots dug into the grass, flattened whole patches—the price of being singled out. And yet the grass came back. Maybe the forest service replanted it every month or season, but you doubt it. Things with roots have tenacity. Living things hold on because life is dear—dear to the grass, dear to the women you watch at the city pool, dear without premeditation.

That resiliency—now that you're fifty, what's interesting about love is the ability to keep loving. After your long-distance nonmonogamous love affair fizzled out, you moved down to

Oakland and after a month, got a job printing for a ritzy department store, I. Magnin, gone out of business now, that had its operation center on the eastern edge of San Francisco, facing the Bay.

It was your first—actually only—foray into corporate life. In Oregon, you learned how to print at a historical society, on an old letterpress—the kind of machine that uses lead type set in lines, one letter at a time. Eventually you convinced the historical society to buy an offset press, a very dinky version of the press this book was printed on. When I. Magnin hired you, it wasn't simply to print, but to be the thirty-four-year-old head of the sign shop for the whole twenty-two store chain.

The best part of working in the sign shop was the view—the windows looked out onto China Basin, where the Giants' stadium is now. Then it was only a room in back of the mail room, which is about as isolated as you can get in a department store chain. Out of sight and thrown the bone of meager authority, you hired another butch—Lois, a fat, African American dyke with a beard and a deep voice. She had no experience, and it was only the two of you in that cramped office looking out at the boats and herons. Sometimes you saw seals, and once, a guy swerved off the tiny bridge and burrowed nose down into the water—heart attack, the police said.

Many kinds of power separated you and Lois, but it was easy to recognize how power separated both of you from everyone else in the building, so you talked, carefully at first. Things you talked about—Buddhism, Judaism, your girlfriends—you never would have talked about with the head of the Advertising Department, whom you taught how to figure out a schedule (you were standing in her office, kind of loving her—all that straight skinny middle-class white girl power she didn't own up to having—and she'd gotten this great San Francisco job—even without the natural insight to count backwards from an event date and figure out if x was needed on y, then it had to be ordered by q. Either you were enlightening her or she was putting you on, probably dead serious, and not too ashamed to ask the printer if no one overheard her). You noticed that even though the ad staff considered you a fashion disaster so extreme as to be an alien from outer space in their midst, you didn't balk about going to the cafeteria to eat lunch at the company subsidized price, sitting alone at a table with a book. Lois wouldn't subject herself to any gaze she didn't have to—she ate in the office, food she brought, often take-out from the night before.

Love for Lois made you quiver, hesitate, fall over your assumptions and struggle to get up. You hired her because an acquaintance who taught a vocational printing class needed to get her a job. When she appeared, no one thought Lois was out of place in the back of the mail room, which was staffed entirely by people of color except for you. The Operation Center was on the other side of town from the main store in Union Square, and while the buyers and ad people were always shuttling back and forth, it was rare for mail room staff to shop there, even with the 20% discount. What were you going to do, blow your paychecks on Gucci scarves? You did buy socks sometimes—the only thing in the store that fit you. And when you could, you'd get those little perfume sample bottles in pretty shapes from the cosmetic staff for your mother and your lover's mother—they always appreciated them.

No one but you knew that Lois could barely print or spell. The sign shop had a big flatbed proof press, on which you laid three-inch plastic letters on metal bars, holding them in place with magnets, and rolled out twenty, fifty signs—for special events or big sales—changing the dates or the prices depending on the store. You ran the small signs (20% OFF   ALL COTTON

SHEETS) on the offset, which was cranky, and gave Lois the big signs to do—they were heavier work, but easier to get right.

Lois couldn't proofread them, though, and sometimes you'd have to scrap a whole afternoon's production and start over because the "e" in Bob Mackie's name was upside down, or the "i" was missing. You thought it was because you grew up reading the *New Yorker* that you could do the job, a middle-class recovering East Coaster who had an attitude about the classes above you. You took to writing, "Help—I'm a prisoner in the evil empire of fashion" on the bathroom walls. But having always taken pride in being efficient, organized and reliable, you did the job you were paid for. Lois was your only subversion.

You were also supposed to supervise the calligrapher, Connie, who had worked for the store for twenty years and hand lettered twenty or thirty—or more—signs a day. She had a separate office over on the advertising side of the hall, away from the noises of the printing presses and mail sorters. Once she told you she was going to a family reunion of all her mother's sisters, who had been in the Japanese internment camp at Tule Lake during the war. "I was only a child then," she said.

"You remember it?"

"Not much."

"Well, have a good time," you said, not knowing what else to say.

"I will." She smiled—indulgently, you thought. You hoped.

You were protective toward Connie, and deferential. She worked, she took care of her mother. Your job was to make sure no one bothered her—the store managers would've had her write every sign if they could, and often you had to turn back five or six times the amount of requests she could reasonably do. The older guys in advertising knew Connie was exploitatively under-paid—"Every sign is a piece of art," they'd whisper, admiringly.

129

You decided that love might also be running interference. But then, you've always been big on distant love.

Loving Connie was easy, though—all you had to do was back off, not make assumptions, and keep her workload as light as possible. Being in the same room with Lois, five days a week, nine to five, love was harder. Lois started having trouble, physical trouble, printing. She'd come in late, and her feet hurt, and she'd botch a batch or two and sit down and groan. "Maybe," you suggested one afternoon, "you should think about different work than printing." Your words twisted in the air and took on a bad smell. Lois stared. You shrugged and went back to work.

Maybe this was after the conversation about Oakland neighborhoods, in which you said "colored kids," meaning kids of color, different kinds, regretting it as soon as it was in the air, even before it was clear you had slapped her in the face. "What did you say?" You could only apologize, completely baffled by the racism you'd soaked up and leaked over her, the sticky underground substance your country pumps into the water and denies, no matter how often you complain about being poisoned. What reason could Lois have to trust you?

Listen, your feet hurt and you were thinking about different work, yourself. You developed plantar fasciitis, which made the soles of your feet cramp, from standing on concrete, and had to have physical therapy, whirlpool baths and massages, three times a week for a couple months. Damned if you were going to let those hot shot ad people see you wince and limp—it was force of will, not physical ability, that got you up the stairs of the building every morning. You didn't tell Lois much about this either—maybe a little, to explain why you did all the sitting work that you could when you were two butches coping with the same pressure in the press room. You meant the suggestion to be that of a comrade in suffering, but that's not what Lois heard. From the shadow that passed over her face and congealed into thunderclouds in her shoulders, you believe she heard, "You shiftless people can't get anything right," but you're guessing.

Lois complained to personnel. She thought they'd be fair, somehow, take her being offended into account, do something for her. What? You didn't have to say anything for personnel to take your side. You were the manager, and no union protected Lois. When you got called upstairs, what they explained was how to arrange her file so you could justify firing her. This shouldn't have surprised you, but it did. "I don't want to fire her," you said. "We'll work it out."

How could you? You were lower class castoffs in the back reaches of the upper class, its servants. You had a fair sense of identity, though you were often self-deluded. Fat, Jewish, smart, competent—they hired you because your resume was grammatically correct and not ink stained, you could pretend to understand the importance of Anne Klein, and you weren't in a union. They actually told you so. You were making more money at thirty-three than you'd ever imagined, but it turned out you had very low expectations for a middle-class kid. Ten dollars an hour seemed like wealth, and you took advantage of the possibilities of being a manager, signing up for printing conferences and bringing in Macintoshes for the print shop and ad room.

But how could you imagine Lois? She came from the nearby Black neighborhood that had been a shipyard during World War II—now among the poorest dumping grounds in the city. She was roughly your size but taller, and everyone who got her on the phone assumed she was a man, from the register of her voice. Jheri curls were popular, and she wore her hair that way, shoulder-length, curly and greased. She had a little mustache and went to Buddhist meetings as an alternative to AA—you could be a Buddhist and still drink, but you had to do it mindfully.

Sometimes she worked as a bouncer at night for gay clubs. She had an active social life and was often worn out at work. Later—after you left the job—you found out she had kidney problems so severe she had to be hospitalized, and you went to visit her in the hospital, clearly surprising her parents.

But that was after you worked it out. Did you work it out? Your lover at that time, Dora, was chronically unemployed, and during busy season—pre-Christmas and the two weeks after—you had money to hire temporary assistants, so you'd drag her into the city to help. She worked hard and smart, and was always after Lois to knock off when you weren't around (resist authority!)—meeting with Connie or the advertising people, going to the store to deliver opera show signs, or talking to your immediate supervisor, a gay man who had absolutely no use in the world for you and was grateful you had none for him, although you did have to consult once in awhile about store promotions or your job review. Dora told Lois she should rebel against capitalism, she should embrace anarchism on the job. You wanted to throw Dora out the window, into the murky slough your building bordered—let her talk anarchism to the harbor seals. Subterfuge was not going to help you and Lois get through.

You were her boss. No two ways around it. You had never been anyone's boss before. Lesbians talk about power in relationships as if the category of lover is different from other ways we negotiate how to get along. It's easier to write how you betrayed your lover or were transformed by letting yourself feel loved than it is to write about finding a way to work it out at work.

When crosses were popular as jewelry, she came in one day with a large crucifix swinging from her left ear. "Lois," you said, trying to figure out how to say *Get that thing out of here,* "I thought you were a Buddhist."

"You mean the earring? It's good, isn't it?"

"Well—"

"You don't like it?"

"It's just that the cross is a powerful symbol."

Lois regarded you warily. "My folks are Baptists."

"I know how important the Black church has been in keeping people together, in helping people have faith—"

"So?"

"Christianity, though—it's the dominant religion. The religion of the government."

Lois started to fiddle with the plastic letters on the rack. "You know I didn't mean anything about your people."

"I know. But it isn't only about being Jewish. It's about how Christians have used Christianity to assimilate people—like in Hawaii, how they made the native Hawaiians ashamed of how they dressed and of their own language, and that made it easier for the big sugar companies to exploit them. And how Christians justified everything they did in Africa by saying they had to convert the heathens and there were slaves in the bible."

Lois fingered the cross. "I wasn't thinking of it like that."

Would you make the same argument to Cornell West? To anyone? Maybe. You've never been anyone's boss the same way since then, and you do like to give these little lectures, even when the power is closer to equal. More than once you've harangued your best friend for wearing lipstick, telling her the story of the tortured rabbits, as if she didn't know.

So you and Lois began conversations about the limits of organized religion, but you had to admit that Buddhism wasn't the same, that chanting didn't hurt anyone. Hell, maybe it helped. You'd admit that.

When you showed your mother around the print shop, and introduced her to Lois, she kept saying what a great thing you'd done for Lois, and this embarrassed you, because you were trying so hard to be a great thing for her without having to admit to a moment of condescension. Some days you could taste Lois's resentment, a metallic taste, as if you were swallowing ink. You developed a theory about the ability to conceptualize abstractly, filling in particulars as they were needed—that language had the coherency of a visual field, and your signs were a series of examples. In this theory, you speculated that Lois couldn't see the whole, only learning case by case, which made it so much harder to remember specifics, to pull up the memory she needed in a particular situation.

Lois navigated the world, and she navigated your silent speculations too—an expert in her own contexts. You made it through about two and a half years together, the length of an average lesbian love affair.

After you handed in your resignation, sometime in the last week you took Lois to an upscale chain restaurant on Fisherman's Wharf that she wanted to try. It was a pleasure, sitting back, two big dykes, looking out at Alcatraz and the Golden Gate. "I want to confess something," Lois said. You waited. "I've got dyslexia—you know what that is?"

"Why didn't you tell me?"

"I was afraid you'd fire me."

"I'm sorry if you thought so. I would have tried to help you in a different way."

"Yeah, I guess you would've."

I couldn't tell if that was exactly what she didn't want, or if she was being wistful for a second chance.

"You know what? You taught me to take pride in my work."

"Yeah?"

"Yeah, thanks."

After that you had a couple dates—going to eat at the soul-food restaurant way down Fourteenth Street, with great candied yams. You heard she went into a detox program, or to a Buddhist retreat. You ran into her a couple times at street fairs. By now, it's been years since you've seen her.

You remember now the self-satisfaction of that meal on Fisherman's Wharf. How you let her thank you and never said thanks back.

DIASPORA

In Tucson, if you whirl around in a circle, you get dizzy on 360 degrees of scenery, your eyes slapping against a mountain peak at every angle. Gerda's been dizzy lately, her daughter Kasha says, but I think it's her medications, or the frustration of being so immobilized after she had to have emergency surgery on the veins in her legs. Kasha's been tending Gerda on and off for the last year, flying into Tucson for open-ended stints. She calls to complain, to tell me I better come. Since my father died last year, I take her seriously.

It's the end of October, and Tucson's still hot. Kasha is talking, talking to me, but I am looking at cactus, at saguaro. Place markers. There is only one saguaro desert in the world. Kasha is talking about the mountains, their names, some way to remember them, north, south, east, west. We're going for lunch downtown. I'm looking at a map, or else I'm driving and she's telling me things about the traffic I already know, things she told me last time we were here together, visiting her mother.

That visit was when we still lived together, while I was working for Macy's, not long after I'd bought the blue pickup, which would make it fall of 1984 or the spring of '85, almost ten years ago. Gerda, Kasha's mother (a woman you would never think to call a "mom"), whom I'd known then about four years, lent me half the money for the truck. After I sent her the first of the monthly hundred dollar repayments, we spoke on the phone.

"Surely you have a friend who needs this money?" she asked. She was smoking then, and I could tell from the soft whoosh I heard that she turned her head sideways to blow the smoke away from the receiver.

"I was thinking the same thing," I said, trying not to let on that when I sent the first $100 check I thought, coals to Newcastle. Coals to Newcastle is an old-fashioned British idiom that most of my friends wouldn't understand. Kasha would and so would Gerda, even though English is her second, maybe third language. She probably learned French first after German. What does coals to Newcastle mean? Sending money to the Rockefellers. Not that Gerda's a Rockefeller.

Gerda's a middle-class German immigrant in her seventies. In the early 1930's when the Nazis forbade Jews to go to college, she was lucky enough to get into America as a student. In 1938, already married to an American, she managed a voyage home, stamped her feet, screamed and yelled, swelled her tiny body with the only tantrum anyone remembers her having, demanded that her family leave. Her father was arrested, yet eventually released after family and friends interceded, when intercession was still possible. It was the small town of Marburg and he still had connections, but prison convinced him that Gerda was right. Her younger sister (who lives in California now, not far from Kasha and me) has another story, because she was left behind to get her mother and brother out, and did, at the last minute, through a combination of luck, cunning, tears and physical determination.

When Gerda lent me the money for the truck, she was a widow with a large savings account. She and her husband had sold their house in Princeton and moved to Arizona for the climate. She kicked him out during their years in Tucson, tired of caretaking, but never divorced. When he died, she refused to follow his instructions for a bequest to his alma mater. "They have enough money," she said. Instead, she gave it to a local organization for the deaf, since he had been deaf since they were in their twenties, and she refused to be acknowledged in their bulletin. When you read "anonymous" in the contributors' list, that's Gerda.

"So," Gerda said to me, "you'll send the money to a friend that needs it?"

"Every month until the loan is paid back."

"But no interest. We don't charge family interest."

"No interest," I said. And sent the money to a dyke in North Carolina every month before I paid the phone bill. Gerda never asked me about it again.

When Kasha and I visited her in that pickup, we had to soak our shirts and bandannas at every rest stop—in fifteen minutes we were roasted dry. It was when I thought springing for air-conditioning in cars was a wasteful bourgeois luxury. Maybe I still think that, but now I'm more comfortable being among the wasteful bourgeoisie.

Her mother's car, the one I'm driving now, has air-conditioning. From the airport we go to eat in a downtown hippie restaurant attached to a renovated hotel, steeped in seediness that tries to be cool and then forgets about its ambition until it almost achieves it. Kasha hasn't held a regular job since she was in her twenties. When we lived together, I finally realized that her mother supported Kasha to keep her for her own use. Kasha says she's so glad I came, Gerda is driving her up the wall, sometimes she has to walk down the street and scream before she can go back and do what ever it is Gerda's demanded—fix some hot chocolate but not too sweet, call the doctors, divide up the pills. "And Harry, that's another thing."

"He's not supposed to come and wipe her ass—he's the boy."

"He could do something. He shows up for a day, talks to the doctors, gets her a prescription for pain meds, and it's like god showed up. She should know better."

"She should, but fear clouds our perceptions."

"Don't take his side."

"I'm not taking his side—I'm taking hers. And yours."

Kasha pushes her black beans around on the plate. "Is it hot in here, or am I flashing?"

"Probably some of both," I said, glad to change the subject to physical misery.

The year Kasha and I drove out here, we went on to Santa Fe to visit friends. On the way back, we drove through Alpine, where Gerda used to come in the summers before she found out the altitude made her lupus worse. Earlier, in the fall of '81, we visited her in that back country, flying into Phoenix and then over the Native lands in a four-seater to the remote mountain town. I remember I came home first, on Yom Kippur when the sun went down. I was alone with the pilot in a tiny plane over northern Arizona, taking snapshots of clouds, and thinking about how Jews find themselves so far from the places they start out.

The first time Gerda and I met, when Kasha and I were on our way west in my old bread van, she insisted I needed a haircut.

"I only let my friends cut my hair," I said.

"Then let me do it."

"Have you ever done it before?" I looked in Gerda's eyes. She had the best eyebrows I'd ever seen—wide, black—like the coats of tiny panthers lying on a ridge below the circle her pinned-up white braids made. She raised one of those black eyebrows, shrugged as if I should know better than to ever doubt her. So I let her.

"Not bad for my first try, if I do say so myself," she said after, surveying my head. Everyone laughed.

Last spring I was about to make reservations to visit Gerda, but then my father died. Kasha went in September and a week—

maybe two—after she got there, after they'd been fighting, and she started to think about coming home for awhile, Gerda got sick—hospital sick. Some terrible pain drove them to the emergency room where Kasha pointed out a discoloration on her mother's leg and they operated at one o'clock in the morning. Her brother, Harry, flew in. Serious. Middle of the night phone calls.

So I thought not to put it off any longer. People die. It was beginning to be clear. Our parents die. Our friends die. Death is always here with us, behind a curtain, under the bed, the monster of childhood, the thing that's going to get us. And it gets us through the people we love, or have been bound with in this life, antagonists, protagonists, old dramas—death is the end, the way the story turns out. The hero and the villain die, the lovers die, the drifter dies, the leader dies, the friend dies while many people hold her, your parent usually dies when you leave the room. My father died in a coma a half hour before visiting hours were going to start again, before we got there. My first lover Ellen's father died when she and her mother left his bedside for coffee.

Gerda is still alive. She's staying reluctantly in the spare room of a young couple because she can't get up and down the stairs into her own apartment, which has a view of Mount Lemon.

"Americans never know how to name things. Lemon. What if we had named the alps Mount Weinershnitzel? As if they asked me." She used to lie on her gray leather couch for hours, watching the pink light change on brown cliffs.

The woman she finds herself relying on now had been her employee, coming in once or twice a week to clean, wash the picture window, move plants, do things Gerda couldn't do for herself. A cheerful, generous woman with problems, whom Gerda counseled as she did her many young friends. Gerda had worked most of her life as a social worker, and she called the people attracted to her as she aged "easy cases." Now the young woman is pleased to give back.

Gerda is ensconced in pillows, framed by the incongruous posters in the room—Marilyn Monroe and the Grateful Dead. Her bed is next to a wood stove, on which Gerda has propped a photo of her two mothers—her birth mother, and the mother who raised her after her birth mother died when she was born. It's a small space that was once the back of the garage, but remade into a guest room, with a door leading in from the carport and another door leading into the dining room. Kasha's been sleeping at the foot of her mother's bed for several weeks on a mat, which is rolled up against one wall now. Gerda is wearing a simple, loose, mid-calf length one-piece dress with long sleeves and a high collar. She could pass for a 1910 cameo. She likes her clothes to be as loose as possible because she also has fibrocitis—which is the catchall phrase for sensitivity in the muscles and skin that doctors can't diagnose more specifically. Every touch is painful to her; even heavily drugged, she finds little physical comfort.

I take the one chair in the room and pull up relatively close—Kasha sits on the edge of the bed, jumping up and down to do errands Gerda requests, or to do anything she can think of to get herself out of the room for a few minutes. The woman whose house it is wants to give Gerda something to eat, but she refuses—she can't, or won't. Since it's almost Halloween, a friend sent a bag of Halloween candy with me—tiny Snickers and Mars bars, which do interest Gerda a little bit, and candy corn which we all agree is too peculiar to be edible.

"Who can eat this?"

"Only seven year olds," Kasha says.

Gerda almost smiles. Then she says, "Did you know, in my town"—she means Marburg, where she came from in Germany—"they always said 'There is a man who has one, but he never shows it'—75 years I've been trying to puzzle out what they meant, what it could have been." She makes a vague gesture in the direction of the photograph of her two mothers. "There is one, who has one, but it's never been seen."

In her town… she must have gone to a Catholic school, since I'd heard stories about knitting scarves or socks or bandages for the missions the nuns ran. She starts to tell the story about bribing her father out of a concentration camp. She and her husband, or was it her sister? Or both? At great risk to themselves. Like the socket where a tooth has been pulled, and nothing put there to replace it, she moves her tongue around the edge of her gum, trying to tell a story about what happened then, but the story is in fragments, the story has been extracted, all that's left to tell is the wound of it, and everyone is bored by wounds. It is not in good taste to talk about your pain, if you can avoid it.

"This shitty thing—" she says in frustration, meaning her leg or stomach or the clothes she's wearing or her relationships with her doctors or the lupus or having to stay in a stranger's house because she would not be carried or left to crawl in an emergency, and refuses to move because it means giving up the view. She separates the t's of shit-ty, through which you can hear her German childhood, the consonant-laden life in the shadow of her father's lumber yard.

Kasha's in the other room. "You know," Gerda says to me, "I used to like listening to Mozart when I really wanted to hear the music, but if I had smoked—"

Gerda was the only person in my parents' generation whom I knew to smoke dope on a regular basis. She occasionally had enough to send her extra to Kasha, and did.

"—if I had smoked, then I wanted that tinkley stuff—oh, you know, give me a word, any word—"

"Baroque? Pre-Raphaelite? Postmodern?"

She gives me a sideways grimace that's half a wink. "Baroque," she says, "or earlier, maybe even that, when I wanted to wrap it around me, and sometimes that awful stuff, sentimental, I could love it or hate it, Schubert—"

She breaks off and I wait. What do I know about this kind of music, this life-long relationship to classical music—active, intellectual and emotional interchange with the structures of sound—me, who only knows from show tunes, a little jazz, and all the silly love lyrics that infect the world now.

"Poetry too," she says, as if she's listening to me and finds a category in which I'm not so out of my depth. "I used to love to read poetry and listen to music. Now I turn it on and I have to turn it right off."

"It used to give you comfort and now it doesn't?" I plod through this thought.

"Yah, I turn it on, and it annoys me or makes me cry. I remember other times. I don't need that. Well, I chalk it up to being a mess, being a mess the last three or four years—"

Kasha comes back into the room with a small white object, and Gerda stops talking about the music. This is the first night Kasha is going to leave her mother. The object turns out to be a baby monitor, which the young couple envision using as a kind of walkie-talkie with Gerda, in case of emergency. Kasha, who is not mechanically inclined, goes back and forth between the rooms five times to make sure it's working.

"You're only procrastinating," her mother says. "You know I want to talk to you about my will. Is that thing turned off? This is only for you and Phyllis to hear."

Kasha sits back on the bed and makes an exasperated face at me, which Gerda cannot see, although she does arch an eyebrow.

144

"So. Everything is all arranged. I had the lawyer make up a trust, and your brother Harry is the executor. The lawyer has the papers, and there's another set in my sewing table."

"Harry!" Kasha is surprised.

"I knew you would get upset."

"If you knew I would get upset, why did you do it?"

"I wanted to make sure you would be okay. And I wanted to ask Phyllis if she would be the back-up person."

"Why don't you think I can take care of myself?"

"I hope you can. I only want to make sure you'll be all right."

"I'm fine. Can't you see I'm fine? I take care of everything, Gerda."

"Stop yelling at me."

"I'm not yelling. Phyllis, am I yelling?"

"Maybe a little," I say.

"I can't believe you're doing this to me," Kasha says, standing up, slamming out the door.

"That went badly," Gerda says, almost wistful. "I thought maybe if you were here—"

"It's all right with me to be the back up, but can I read it first?"

"Yah, sure, Kasha knows where my sewing drawer is. Tell her to show it to you tonight. I always think she won't be so fragile."

"I don't think she is so fragile. You surprised her, that's all. And she wants you to appreciate her competency, tell her she's doing a good job."

"She doesn't know?" Both of Gerda's eyebrows go up.

"I know you think she should, but she doesn't. Maybe you could tell her."

"She should know." Gerda is looking at something far away from this room. "If I have to say it, then it becomes a matter of form, not from the heart." She makes a small circular gesture, "It's humiliating."

I touch Gerda's hand lightly. "Don't worry. Kasha's fine. She's just a very expressive woman."

"I don't know how I got such an American child," Gerda says. "God, I wish I could smoke. Or have a martini. It gave me rashes, did you know?"

"Drinking or smoking?"

"Oh, who knows? Drinking, the doctors said. Those rashes— I don't think much of vanity but there's a certain way you are supposed to present yourself to the world. I can wish, though, can't I?"

"If wishes were horses—."

Gerda smiles. "Go on, you go get her and get some sleep. I don't want to talk about this anymore tonight. I'll see you in the morning."

When we get to Gerda's apartment, Kasha cries. "Why can't she manage to say thank you? Is that so hard? Thank you?"

"She does say thank you."

"Only formally, like, thank you for the newspaper. That's not it."

"I know what you mean, Kasha, but she can't. She wants you to know how much she loves and needs you, and if she tells you, it embarrasses her."

"And what about me? You don't think it embarrasses me that she doesn't think I can manage my own life? That she has to call in goddamn Harry?"

"You know, let me look at the papers." While Kasha finds them, I put on a tape of something by Bach that was next to the stereo system.

"Your mother says she can't listen to music anymore, it makes her too unhappy."

146

"That's bullshit," Kasha says, coming back with the papers.

"How come?"

"I don't know—she always has some psychoanalytic explanation for everything."

"You don't think it's true?"

"It probably is. Maybe I'm jealous she told you."

"Don't be—you're the one she cares about." I'm trying to read the fine print quickly. "Look," I say, "I don't know why she made this will thing seem so dramatic, but the way it's written leaves you the option of firing Harry whenever you want."

"It does?"

"Yeah, it's a loophole big enough to drive a truck through. I think she wants you two to have each other when she's gone."

"Well, she could say that."

"Clearly she can't."

"But why does she have to be so judgmental with it?"

"I think—"

"What?" Kasha is pacing the room, picking up objects—small Navajo pottery bowls, ashtrays—and putting them down.

"I think you're what's keeping her here."

"What do you mean?"

"Here on this plane. Worrying about you, making this estate stuff into a soap opera—it's what's left that keeps her connected."

"Maybe," Kasha says.

"It's going to be all right."

She sits next to me and breaks out in long gulping sobs. "Why doesn't she say she loves me?"

"Oh, Kasha, she loves you so much."

"Did she tell you that?"

"Yes, actually."

"Why can't she tell me?"

"I told you."

"You always understand her better than I do."

"We recognize each other, your mother and I, that's all."

"I wish she would recognize me."

"She can't, you're too close to her. But she loves you, don't doubt it."

Kasha rubs the tears off her face. "I know she does."

"C'mon, let's try to get some sleep."

Around six-thirty A.M., the phone rings. It's the young woman, saying Gerda's in the emergency room again. We get there as quickly as we can. When Kasha comes out, she says that Gerda insists her angina started up with the argument about the will. "She said anything could start it, any stress. Is she blaming me?"

"She's very good," I say.

"You think she did this on purpose?"

"No, not at all. But I think she's using it, since it did happen. She wants to make sure you don't get mad and go. And she missed you last night."

"She could ask me to stay."

"You're mother thinks asking for what she needs is a sign of weakness."

"That must be why you understand her." Kasha kicks at some dust on the floor.

"Being butch and being German are a little different." Kasha isn't paying enough attention to be amused. I put my hand on her arm. "Is she out of danger?"

"Yes, the doctor thinks so. But they're keeping her a couple hours for observation."

"Then let's go for a ride. Since I have to go home tomorrow, we should take the opportunity."

Against a high bluff in Saguaro Canyon, a giant cactus makes a U with its bent arms, as if to hold the sky. A sliver of white moon moves against the blue. I watch it disappear behind the rock as Kasha walks to the stream and dips her Jewish star in. I wonder what Germany looks like, if Gerda's town had mountains.

It's exactly Halloween the night I fly back, and the stewardesses are dressed in costumes, holding silly contests among the passengers. A prize for the passenger with the most keys, for the passenger who can connect an old advertising slogan to a particular product. My guess about how many peanuts the airline serves in a year is closest to accurate, and I win a pair of Groucho Marx glasses—fake eyebrows and big nose—which I wear, disembarking.

ANTELOPE

Between the streaks of dirt on the Greyhound bus window, Phyllis could see the mottled western landscape, as if the ground were the face of a wart hog turned upward, loving its reflection in the sky. A small group of running animals—not deer, what? streaked through the grayish green stubble. Antelope? She pressed as close to the greasy window as she dared. Too small for elk, and definitely not deer—she had seen enough deer through the chain-link fences of zoo parks her father had taken her to as a child to know what deer looked like. They must be antelope. "Where the deer and the antelope play..." The animals disappeared behind what would be a mesa in a couple hundred or a thousand years. She leaned back against the bus seat headrest and turned to look at her sleeping lover.

No, they were in the car, that first Chevy wagon they owned, on their way to Chicago from Portland, passing Little America, the world's biggest truck stop, and it was 1968. Her lover was driving, and Phyllis turned to see the antelope herd. Angry as she was—no, she was not angry yet, that was another trip—young as she was (yes, she was definitely young; they were eating peanut butter and jelly sandwiches, listening to AM radio, stopping at campgrounds and listening to the stories of women who washed their children's clothes in the campground bathrooms, grateful that they could not see their own fate in those moody white faces), she was learning to appreciate this sense of hooves across a vast space, this quick grazing leap which promised wilderness somewhere beyond what she could see. In the after-image of the antelope, America was still a country with a network of tribes who had not tracked every river and valley, who knew enough not to build highways, whose maps were songs and petroglyphs. America—the world—was an expanse that was not yet parceled and owned, and in it the animals thrived without schedule.

She did not mind that now, 31 years later, although she had crossed the country maybe ten times, she remembered the journey rolling out on the other side of dirty bus windows. It's easy to remember stopping at night in some small station, the way you note the travelers on the way with you—how poverty and fear, certain kinds of loss mark them. Once she had been on the bus from New Orleans to Biloxi, before Biloxi had casinos, and a man said to the bus driver, "I had a wife and kids, a job. Now I go from bus to bus." He was a white man in dark clothes that were too big for him, too hot for the weather. He didn't smell, or she was far enough away not to notice the smell, although she could hear him as clearly as Woody Guthrie songs on the old 50-buck phonograph she had in high school—scratchy, the treble too high.

"So long, so long, gotta travel on"—isn't this what happens to people in the U.S.? So much country without borders—it gives us all a sense of entitled motion. What was Phyllis doing going to Biloxi, anyway? Their motel was on the Gulf of Mexico—at night, the crabbers went out at low tide, with nets and lights held high. The lights moved among black pillars over the sheen of dark water. Phyllis drew something in the sand. Her 13th lover rubbed it out. "Who asked you for romance?" Then her lover laughed, as if it were a joke, nothing to worry about.

They had stolen the plane tickets. Scammed them. In the 1970s, various fringe communities passed around ways to get things for free: corporate calling card accounts, ways to order tickets from the airlines as Dr. Jones—some name close enough to your own that if photo ID was asked for at the airport (which it wasn't then, but in case it was), you could say there was a typo, some small mistake. You ordered the tickets sent to the address of someone who was about to move, and everyone knew someone about to move in the '70s, so that when the bill came, no one had a clue whom it was for. The airlines wised up. Everyone got credit cards or had to go down with cash to their local office. Wasn't it coming anyway? Small town courtesies extended by corporations were a momentary aberration. Phyllis and her lover Thorn went to New Orleans by seizing the moment of aberration. They congratulated each other on their daring, the way they made their luck by simply believing in it.

They stayed in a gay guest house and drank Bloody Marys; they met some local dykes in a bar who were both hospitable and suspicious of northerners, but Phyllis was slightly infamous at the time as the author of quirky radical articles, and they were invited to spend a night or two in someone's home. Phyllis and Thorn hadn't been lovers for more than two months, originally attracted to each other by the seriousness of work they did for a big lesbian conference. They were white lesbians; Phyllis a Jew, Thorn an atheist from Christian background. They had both been locked up in mental institutions: Phyllis managed to get out with only minor residual drug damage to her nervous system, but Thorn had been shocked out of half her memory.

She thinks about Thorn. It's been more than twenty years since she even heard her voice, got a letter. Is Thorn alive? At the end Thorn said, "If you ever use my story, I swear I'll track you down and—" But it's her own story that she wants to tell, to remember. Half of the story belongs to her. Can you rip the story in two, like an old photograph, removing the one you don't want, cutting the torn edge to a smooth strip: *it was just me? I was the one watching the crabbers out on the Gulf; I went back to New Orleans after we had an argument on the bus about the wisdom of age. I was three years older, which meant a lot to me for reasons which Thorn hated. She was right. We lay together on a mattress on the floor in a lesbian's home in New Orleans and I thought: here is the place where the seed of our end is planted.*

Can she tell that? She was looking out the bus windows as they came back into New Orleans. A man had given everything up and couldn't go back; his grief was a light leaking out towards the horizon. Phyllis had an analysis of men, of men's privilege, even in giving things up, walking away from their homes and families, following some vision of personal tragedy. It was never safe for women to renounce their lives, unless they could go to nunneries or had money. The few women on the streets die faster than men. Everyone knows that.

She had always been puzzled by the people who do studies to prove what everyone knows. Everyone knows: that racism destroys lives; that men oppress women; that the antelope are almost gone in the United States. As she got older, she conceded the wisdom of entering arguments with statistics. Usually people like to believe that things are better, that progress is good for them, that time is on their side and individuals can do anything with their lives. Your life is a dollar and everyone supposedly gets the same dollar—you can save it, spend it, teach it to turn cartwheels in the air, and ignore the fact that someone is always trying to pick your pocket. So it's important to know where your wallet is and have some statistics memorized to back you up.

Everyone also knows: lesbian relationships don't last long. She knows this even though she's been with her current lover for twelve years. But before that, two and a half years was average, if you don't count the short affairs, a day to about three months. Sex is, after all, not a relationship. But not sex is not not a relationship either. (Phyllis loves the double negative, the sideways affirmation. Thorn despised that about her, which years after the fact Phyllis decided was anti-Semitism on Thorn's part.) She still E-mails her first lover, the one with whom she ate peanut butter and jelly and watched the antelopes. They have been friends for thirty-three years now, dating from when they first knew each other in high school.

Thorn said, "If you think you're going to get that from me after we break up, you're wrong. I'm not sitting around some diner reading the daily paper with you in companionable silence like your other ex-lovers." She said "companionable" with a sneer. Phyllis stayed friends with almost everyone, certainly with everyone she'd been with for more or less two and a half years, except for Thorn, who disappeared. It has often seemed to Phyllis that the whole point of the drama—getting into sex and then ending it—is to be able to read the paper, the books, the articles, the poems together, fitting the interesting bits into a mosaic of what's said out loud. It's possible that what she was searching for at twenty-five was not love but language. Thorn would have said, "Then why don't you say something worthwhile?"

Somewhere she has a photograph of the first morning they were in New Orleans, drinking Bloody Marys at a patio cafe in the French Quarter. Thorn has a dark streak through her left eyelid, a visible blue vein. It was the pulsing of that vein that Phyllis found so attractive in Thorn's long, serious face. Thorn believed that if Phyllis only concentrated, she could control her power. If she could control her power, there was no telling what she might be able to do. She might be able to stretch her hands over Thorn's shocked head and restore the burnt connections.

An image shows up in her mind, but is it her own memory? Phyllis believes it is, but is not sure. Perhaps she saw a photograph of it in a magazine; the image-fingers with a spark of blue light arcing across them. They made a spark like that between them when they first got together, once. Or else it never happened, and

155

they each had read about it and thought if anyone could perform this feat, it had to be them, representatives of the greatest emotional intelligences to ever grace the planet, lesbians. Phyllis found herself backing down, unsure she was up to what Thorn wanted, nervous about what Thorn would want next if she could perform the first miracle.

Miracles are, after all, only ideas, and both of them had the idea that Phyllis could heal Thorn. She had strong, blunt hands and she put them to use between Thorn's legs. Everyone knows: what men have damaged, lesbians can fix. Or do only lesbians know this? When will, intuition and patience failed Phyllis, and Phyllis failed to heal Thorn, she decided only money would work: a regular job, a mortgage, weekends in the Green Mountains.

First Thorn was scornful, then she started to hit. Phyllis was bigger; she had been in dyke patrol. Thorn smashed her in the arm, the side of the neck. Only after three or four blows did Phyllis remember she had learned how to block. She blocked, and Thorn punched her arm. "Leave me alone," Thorn said, and slammed her door. Sometimes Phyllis would leave then for a couple hours or drive to Marblehead for the weekend. This was five or six years before battering was talked about among lesbians. Phyllis believed that Thorn's violence came from the physical damage that had been done to her, and so she tried to ignore it. Likely that infuriated Thorn, but this is not Thorn's story, is it?

In Phyllis's story, a friend says to her, years later, "She never hit anyone else, did she? She never hit you in public. She had more aim than you're giving her credit for." Thorn said, "I know you're selfish, I know you're limited, I know you're afraid. Later, women will love you again but only I will know what a fake you are, how you refuse to live up to what you know you can be."

Phyllis wept. They were driving away from somewhere and she glanced over at the map after Thorn gave her directions.

"That's what I mean—you don't trust me. You can't trust me. If you were really my partner, you'd never check up on me, you'd never want to see the map. You're bullshit."

Phyllis pulled over to the side of the road. "I only—" No way to say, no way to know, then, that she'd do the same thing at forty, at fifty—glance over her right shoulder even when her lover says, "All clear on the right." Is it only a question of getting the right lover, the one who is only minimally annoyed by this, who brings it up to share a joke about control, not shame her about trust?

How did it end up being this story? Phyllis had a first lover and she has a last lover, with both of whom she has driven across America twice. She meant to keep on about the antelopes, how once she had seen a whole herd of them, from the highway. Now, at the turn of the millennium, if you drive back roads in Nevada or Texas, places where dry country dips and stretches its upper arms in the sun, you might see one or two.

She also saw a deer once, with a full rack of antlers, staring into her face from an icy ledge in the Cascade Mountains. She was on the cross country train, going to Portland, where Thorn believed a doctor offered hope. Phyllis stared at the deer, at the ledge, the fir branches holding the snow in their arms like gifts, until it was out of sight.

The doctor they took the train to see ran tests. For some reason, they had to stay up all night at a bowling alley. Phyllis had been in Portland before, and now (or then) she realized that cities you've lived in get cobbled together to become a dream landscape—here's the curve of rock as you come out of the Portland hills merging with Clark Street in Chicago, where the 23-hour a day movie theater was, that only closed to change the double feature around five a.m., and clear the seats of drunks. For a quarter extra, you could sit in the ladies' balcony, no men allowed. Phyllis liked to sit up close at the movies, so she learned the hard way about the move she called "the Chicago feel," even though she knew men do it in every city. Her father had done it, once, when she was sixteen, but because he didn't have the requisite raincoat, she was almost unsure what his hand on her knee meant.

Often she is in this collage landscape—Chicago, Portland, New Orleans, Northampton, Old San Juan, Atlanta, Boulder— and it's a short walk to the beach where a tidal wave is coming in. Sometimes, before the tidal wave, she's lucky: otters, whales, seals with their cautious black eyes looking sideways, fill the water. She knows then that she's been blessed. Animals come to her in dreams, the deer watches from its ledge, the owl spreads its wings when she is alone in the forest, a bear cub stares at her and her new lover the morning they wake up on the Elk River, stares, and is gone. These sightings have no consequences besides a full heart.

Thorn said to the doctor, "Your technician raped me."

"What did you say?"

"He raped me. He stuck that tube up my nose at four a.m., and when I said it hurt, he shoved harder."

The doctor was relieved. The ordinary sadism of lab technicians is not rape. He tried to get Thorn to see her exaggeration for what it was.

Thorn walked out.

Phyllis stared at the doctor. They had come all this way. When they crossed the Plains, the compartment they were in had no heat, and only a handful of blankets. Thorn gave her blanket to a young girl. The deer had looked Phyllis in the eye. "But you can see how it was an abuse of power?" She asked tentatively. Suppose Thorn wanted to come back, suppose this doctor did have an answer?

Thorn came back in and grabbed her hand. "Traitor," she said in the hall. Phyllis said something to defend herself, but she knew Thorn was right. She was slow to react to men, to anyone, who had blown their chance. Phyllis was always going around giving people the benefit of the doubt, looking for the other side, as if that would somehow insulate her from brutality.

Later they were at the beach, that place on the Oregon coast where a surviving remnant island not more than twenty irregular feet wide sits in a lagoon and a small cypress tree grows out of its craggy top. Anytime it appeared in a dream, you'd recognize it. In their beach motel Thorn made love to Phyllis; she let Thorn do it, even though she didn't want to. She was angry, disappointed. She suffered touch and pretended it was sufficient, because she could not ask for an apology, and Thorn could not say, "Sorry." This is where I have finally done you wrong, Phyllis thought, *and you don't know it.*

And you don't know it. But what if Thorn did know? It's not her story. It's Phyllis's. One day not long after they got back to the East Coast, they were going to the races at the county fair. Before they left the house, they argued about betting. It was Thorn's position that if they concentrated, they could not fail. "Haven't we been failing?" Phyllis wanted to know. Thorn hauled off and punched her in the eye. Phyllis turned at the last minute and caught the blow on the bone instead of in the soft socket, otherwise that eye would be gone.

Later, when Phyllis was living alone in the old bread truck that had been converted into a homemade RV by a shop teacher, she would sometimes stop at county fairs and make two-dollar bets. She rarely lost more than twenty bucks. She likes county fairs, likes to wander the aisles where the sheep, goats and baby pigs are, and now they have llamas too, around which you have to be careful, because they like to spit. The cattle stalls disturb her, with the young white kids brushing the heifers, talking sadly about how much they will be forced to get for them a pound.

She had a first lover, she has a lasting lover, she had lovers in between. In the middle of the list Phyllis sometimes goes over, Thorn leans back, relaxed, at a table in the sunlight in New Orleans, laughing. The antelope kick up dust and are mostly gone. Phyllis knows there's an easy way out of this—blame the enemy, who is man. Man who lays asphalt on the sweating brow of the Mojave desert and sucks the Colorado River dry, man who decides the brain is a pair of dice and you can shock it sideways in a gamble for a better roll.

Who wouldn't want an answer that places the blame squarely outside of the way you behaved? Some things can't be resolved, not by living long enough, not by art. Children leave home and don't come back; a foot is lost to frostbite or gangrene; it's possible to glue broken pieces back together, but you will always see the crack. The fact is when Phyllis imagines the photograph torn in half, she's the one who's missing, not Thorn. The refuge of a battered dyke is to believe that your lover was right; you could have been: more honest, clear, brave, trusting, intuitive, sincere. You were given a chance to have true love, but what you did instead was grow up, accepting that it would not be you who save the antelope.

THE MOTH

When the moth appeared, we were watching a movie about a dying grandmother. I happened to know the filmmaker was a lesbian—twenty years ago the women's movement film co-op I worked for distributed her first short film. But you wouldn't have guessed she was a dyke from this movie, which a friend had taped off of cable.

This filmmaker was funny, creative, Jewish, loving. But the film stayed completely focused on her grandmother. On cable, lesbians are only allowed to deal with one issue at a time—no sidebars on social justice issues. Around the scene where the film-maker and her mom go to Grandma's sickbed to see if they can learn her gefilte fish recipe, this lemon-colored moth brushed through our hallway door frame.

"Oh," I said, startled, "it's huge."

"You call that huge? It's smaller than your fist. That's not huge." Fanny smiled at me, the skin around her mouth smoothing in a sweet stretch, playful, quick and easy.

"Just because it's not Mothra—"

"Yeah, Mothra." She was laughing, about to tickle me, but our attention was pulled back to the television by a sigh from Grandma.

We nestled up, glad to have this video instead of watching "Wheel of Fortune," which we often do while eating dinner on the couch. Sometimes I hear the ghost of Pauline Newman, the great Progressive Era labor organizer, whispering mournfully, "We fought so hard for those hours and they waste them. We used to

161

read Tolstoy, Dickens, Shelley, by candlelight and they watch the 'Hollywood Squares.' Well, they're free to do what they want. That's what we fought for."

I stared Pauline's disapproval down while Fanny rubbed my arm. Fanny has to get to bed by nine since she's up at five a.m., girding herself for the commute. Ever since I worked swing-shift as a typesetter, I can't get to sleep before two; these hours of evening overlap were like honeysuckle—a little sticky, irresistible.

After Fanny had been asleep for four or five hours, I came to bed as usual. I turned the light out and closed my eyes. In another room, something fell or hit the screen. A car braked too hard on the highway. I was nearly asleep when I heard a noise I couldn't identify—scratchy, breathy. In the room? Overhead? Outside? Someone breaking into our cars?

The window behind our heads is covered by a slatted metal shade—I reached up and pulled it away from the glass. Up at the top, between the shade and the window, the moth was beating its wings.

White light filtered into the bedroom from our dusk-to-dawn front porch light that's so bright I sometimes wear a mask to sleep. The moth was trying to get to it through the glass. I thought about getting up, going into the kitchen for a container, trapping the moth and letting it out. But I'd have to stand on the bed and wake Fanny. I'd have to actually move away from that two a.m. sensation sucking me into the mattress. Even so, I considered opening the window. I only open it on the hottest nights because the freeway noise pours in stronger than the porch light. I don't mind the noise and the light, really. It's the city, it's our new little house on a short street in the urban outskirts three blocks from the freeway—I like it fine. But the front windows have sliding glass panels that open on screens. You can't slide them and shoo a moth out.

So I lay there, listening to it beat its wings. Was it suffering? Do moths suffer, trapped inside? Do they panic? Do they beat themselves to death against the obstruction that keeps them from burning? Did it want the light or simply the wind, the green night beyond us?

I am going to fall asleep, I thought, *while this moth beats against the window.* This is another of all the things I sleep through, all the needs of specific people, not only the raped women of Serbo-Croatia, not only the Jews who got blown up in Argentina this week nor the Palestinians driven from their homes, not the factory workers in Indonesia who get $1.80 for a ten-hour day, but my friends, women I've met and care about, women I know who need medical care, help getting through school, money for rent. *I'm closing my eyes and going to sleep.*

And I did.

In the morning, the alarm rang and Fanny came in, so it must have been Saturday morning, since she wasn't at work. She lay beside me. I asked her if she loved me anyway.

"Anyway what?"

"Anyway because I haven't changed the world yet."

"You're asking a rhetorical question." She rubbed her knuckles softly against my cheek. "You know, I remember when we learned about rhetorical questions at school. They fascinated me. The idea that something could be designed to not be what it appeared to be, and that there was a name for it, a way to study it—I thought that was amazing."

She had a pink rapture in her face. The idea of a rhetorical question never gave me a moment's pause. Of course people manipulate you with their language. Traps are everywhere, aren't they? But for her, the forethought, the intent, to lead someone on while making them think they were engaged in conversation, a give and take, was dramatic. A revelation.

"If I ever write a book about you, I'll start it with that," I said, filling with the pleasurable sensation of her seriousness.

"You'll forget."

"No I won't. I don't forget. I didn't forget about the moth."

"What moth?"

"The one that was caught between the shade and the window last night."

She raised the shade to look. "No moth here—it must have found a way out."

That moment the moth fell from a corner of the molding and landed on my elbow. I didn't move. Moths don't bite or crawl across your face with sharp hairy legs like spiders. But I did make some kind of sound. So did Fanny. Moths only speak to people with their wings. I thought one of hers crunched when Fanny picked her up and took her outside.

"I put her on the hedge by the door," Fanny said. "She's happy now."

KNAYDLE AND
THE LIBRARIAN

Shayna is waiting for Knaydle. The blue jeans and shirt she wears to her job as librarian at Legal Aid won't do today. She dresses thoughtfully—soft salmon pink blouse, tailored brown slacks. She rubs her hands across the pleats at the top of her thighs. These glass earrings match, she thinks, holding them up to her ears in front of the mirror, the pale yellow pulling the morning's translucence into her dark face. She fastens a thin gold chain to drape below the well at the base of her neck, patting her chest. Librarians, after all, are good with details.

Knaydle is round and wet but chewy. If the moon were butch, she'd be Knaydle—busy trying to define the horizon, self-important, patching together fog in order to hide her sentimentality but steady for all that, comforting as she moves across your sky. Knaydle has been taking a break, renting space in the country, setting out her watercolors to find the patience to paint an acorn woodpecker. This summer she was laid off of her night job doing newspaper paste-up, and had persuaded another dyke to take over her position as coordinator of the local lesbian-save-the-world committee for seven weeks.

She loves being alone in the country, where a deer might leap across the road in front of her, a fox streak out of the range of her headlights. Sometimes she knows the animals will appear before she sees them, and in those rare moments of connection, she has the experience of spiritual awe—not that she would ever describe it that way when her friends ask if, perhaps, she isn't bored during all those nights alone. Still, a few meetings in the city can't be avoided, and she longs for her lover as otters long for abalone. Summer stickiness is approaching in the middle of the West Coast states. Knaydle throws her laundry in the back of her pickup truck and drives the three hours into town, directly to Shayna's.

After two years, Knaydle has formed a romantic vision of her relationship with Shayna that parallels her Hebrew school knowledge of the early kibbutz movement—purposeful, pleasurable days in which the desert bloomed and brought forth fruit, evenings full of thoughtful discussion, sensitive and sensual talking while they ate the pulp of warm oranges (and in that fantasy, no land had been appropriated, no one displaced for the sake of an ideal). Her ex-lovers find Knaydle's enthusiasm for the librarian hard to fathom. They see a tall, bookish, serious, kind woman— the one who seeks the most ill-at-ease newcomer at a party to welcome in—a proper, earnest sort of woman, easy to surprise. Before Shayna, Knaydle had gone for either drama queens or adventurous rebels—dope-smoking half-burnt out activists who didn't know what they wanted to do when they grew up, but were worldly wise. Shayna is orderly, organized, often shy, and completely unshakable in a conversation about principles—so convinced about what is right and wrong that Knaydle's ex's think Shayna a little, well, naive.

Finally pulling up in front of Shayna's apartment, Knaydle takes a moment of pleasure in her excellent parallel parking job. Hot from the road, she slings her bag of dirty clothes over her shoulder and cradles a dozen red roses carefully in her arm, hoping they'll catch Shayna's attention before the stains on her old T-shirt do. Knaydle moves her short, wide body through the world by force of will, trying to make her presence imply she has the right, the same right as anyone to fight for what she believes, swim in any pool, rub her hand's across a woman's skin. But under this force of will, she worries and sighs: how is it possible to have ended up happy, a fat Jewish girl from Long Island?

Shayna opens the door with the intent look of a girl carefully untying a ribbon on a giant birthday present. Knaydle stares at her salmon colored blouse (ironed, too), wishing she could raise an eyebrow, settling on bending her head forty-five degrees to angle a kiss on Shayna's cheek. Shayna grabs Knaydle's shoulder and Knaydle, drawn in, pulls away—only an hour and a half for the laundry, for reporting on everything.

"Alright, put your laundry in while I arrange the roses." Shayna says, hugging Knaydle to her breasts. "While you're downstairs, guess what I'm wearing underneath this."

Knaydle tries to imagine, positioning quarters in the washing machine slot, amazed that here in Oakland a woman would greet her this way, because after all there's that fine line between coming off as a butch or a shlub. Upstairs the roses fill Shayna's purple glass vase, made for this. "A lover," Knaydle says, struggling for composure (and breath, after bolting upstairs), "should always have a vase handy for roses."

"Just in case," Shayna agrees and then they are embracing. Knaydle opens her eyes in sensual shock and closes them as their lips fit, press, puzzle over each other and remember the answer again. Knaydle takes Shayna's hand off her jeans and molds its palm to her cheek, surprised by desire.

"Did I make a mistake?" Shayna asks, laughing, but a little unsure underneath, her uncertainty a faint blush under her olive skin. "Aren't you my lover? Don't we do this?"

"Oh, we do." Knaydle takes a deep breath, then moves her hand to the bottom of Shayna's pants and very slowly works the top button loose, tugs the zipper slowly down—a little bit of blouse is caught, uncaught. "Maybe you're not wearing anything," Knaydle says. Then she sees the black lace—Shayna's garter belt, her stockings, the small bikini butterfly lace underwear Knaydle gave her for their first month anniversary, laughing about how none of their friends would ever suspect.

Knaydle presses Shayna's belly with the flat of her palm, listening to her lover suck in her breath. Shayna's belly is soft and quivers. Knaydle grabs the top of the black underwear and pulls up on it sharply, so Shayna can feel the pressure, the thin line of lace taut against the ruffled outer lips, hard as it trails across her anus.

They start for the bedroom. Shayna's slacks rest open, held up by the fullness of her hips. Knaydle experiences a rush of pleasure at how well those pants fit, the neatness of the ironed crease. Now she relaxes and expands into her own flesh, excited. She stops Shayna in the hall, pushes her up against the plaster. Shayna leans back. "Here?"

Knaydle doesn't answer. Right outside the kitchen doorway, she pulls Shayna's pants down, moving down with them, crouching on her knees. Then she reaches up to roll the lace underwear down Shayna's thighs to the top of her stockings where the garters are fastened. Bracing herself with one hand, she can just manage to use the other to pull Shayna's outer lips open. Knaydle falls forward into that inner layering and tongues Shayna's clitoris, which swells as she slumps and tries to hold herself up against the wall.

"I know what I want for my 50th birthday," Shayna's voice had dropped an octave, and she's wheedling.

"What?" Knaydale manages quickly, sucking a breath.

"More of this."

Pulling her, pushing her more firmly against the wall, Knaydle tries a longer whisper, "You're a slut." She moves back an inch to make sure Shayna heard. She watches her lover's bright green eyes disappear behind fluttering eyelids. Knaydle continues, very softly, very low, "You dress like this to make me take you.

168

Where do you want to be taken? On the kitchen floor? In the hall? You can't wait, can you?"

"No," Shayna's breath catches in her throat.

Then she says, "Yes," but Knaydle can't keep it up, not the soft core dirty talking or the licking, while crouching on her knees. She sits, but sitting she's too short to reach where Shayna's long legs soften and pinnacle at her sex. "My shoes," Shayna says.

Knaydle slips Shayna's feet free of the pumps, pulls Shayna's pants all the way down and off, runs her hand in a hungry sweep along the stockings from thigh to feet, sweet slinky sensation of rub and tension crackling. She squeezes the tip of Shayna's toes but still, bunched on the floor looking up at Shayna's garter belt, can't quite reach.

"Let's go to the bed," Shayna pleads.

"Wait." Under the telephone table, there's a neat stack of phone books—and luckily, Oakland is a big city. Knaydle perches on both the yellow and white pages.

Shayna laughs, "How come in all the lesbian sex stories it's always a perfect fit?"

"Because we don't write them," Knaydle says, now pulling Shayna back, pulling her vagina toward her mouth. Shayna's bleeding. Knaydle pushes the little tampon string down, out of the way. After two years, they believe they have nothing danger-ous, though they are remotely aware of how they're pressing their luck.

"I hope I don't taste like soap," Shayna worries, "having washed for you."

"No, you taste clean—you taste like sex." Knaydle licks with her long strong tongue, circling, switching the membrane back and forth.

"I can't," Shayna moans. Her knees are buckling, trembling. "You're making me weak in the knees." They each suppress a giggle.

"No more clichés," Knaydle slaps Shayna's thigh lightly. "This is what you asked for, slut—you can stand it a little longer." She moves her tongue through flesh for another minute even as Shayna's wilting on her feet.

The bed is covered with library books and crossword puzzles, as if Shayna hadn't imagined that the seduction she'd so carefully prepared would occur. Now she sweeps everything onto the floor and rummages through the bedside table drawer, searching for the lubricant. She places the black bottle by the pillow as she lies down. Knaydle quickly pulls off her pants and shirt, leaving on a black undershirt, purple underwear.

"Who did you dress for?" Shayna laughs, grabbing for her. Knaydle sloshes beside Shayna on the waterbed, unsnapping the garters so she can slip the lace underwear off. All the garters are easy except the last one, which is behind her leg. Knaydle can't see it but finally the elastic pops back, tingles Shayna's skin.

"That felt good," Shayna whispers.

Grinning, Knaydle finally gets the butterfly off so Shayna can spread. She takes a deep breath and exhales, feeling fat and strong beside Shayna's length. "You know how big I am, how wide you have to open to let me in," she murmurs, pulling both of Shayna's breasts from her velour sports bra while hooking one leg over Shayna's thigh. Knaydle sucks on Shayna's exposed nipples, presses against her, takes the nipple deep in her mouth, making it harden, pucker and rise. She alternates between mouth kisses and nipple sucking as she rubs and pats Shayna's cunt. Kissing, rubbing, she closes her eyes and sees that in their flesh reside all the secrets of the Kabala, written in lesbian code. She wonders if later, alone, it would be possible to make a painting of the intricate patterns their bodies reveal.

"I want you sitting between my legs," Shayna says, and Knaydle forgets about the painting, rolls on her side and shifts her weight until she's in place, caressing, rubbing, slapping Shayna's thighs, cooling her clitoris with the wet lubricant. As she sits, Knaydle pulls her tank top up, so her vast breasts rest on Shayna's legs, brushing the crease of her belly and cunt. Shayna curves her hand around Knaydle's left breast, making a throaty sound of satisfaction.

Now Knaydle is concentrating. She gets two fingers in along side the tampon which surprises Shayna, who inhales sharply. Knaydle slows, looking for any sign that it might be too much, but Shayna pushes on her breast and sighs, "more more   more." Knaydle rubs her cunt with two fingers, while pushing in with the other hand. The tension strains her back and she shifts, wishing for a wall to lean against, uncomfortable struggling for position against the undulating surface of the bed—the only hitch in this, but not anything that she'd let stop her.

Talking helps her focus on Shayna. "Take more—you know you've been wanting this. Everyone thinks you're so proper, so refined, but I know better. You're not just my girl…" Knaydle stops breathing for a second, overwhelmed by the bright gray sensation of doing this, saying these words, then exhales, slightly dizzy, intent—"You're my slut and the more you want, the more I'm going to make you take. I'm not going to stop, not going to let up. You have to take more. Take more." Shayna groans and writhes, arches, widens and then her legs tighten.

Pulling her fingers out, Knaydle holds Shayna's cunt open with one hand, keeps rubbing Shayna's clit with two fingers of the other. Shayna stays tight and Knaydle feels a film cover her face, her eyes—now she has the sensation that a deer will materialize beside them, as she had two days ago driving on Route 20 just before a deer ran across the slope above the road. As she stares into her memory of the deer's face, her lover comes.

Shayna pulls her whole body up—the muscles clamp spasm clamp she sits up her mouth opens but only a small oh escapes and then a longer one she leans back rises again oh oh all the gush of wind in the body wind and liquid running pushing at the boundaries. Knaydle laughs, pleased with herself, maneuvering back at last to lie against Shayna's side. A little fussy, she reaches for a tissue to wipe the juice and blood and lubricant off her hand before wrapping an arm around her lover.

Often Shayna falls asleep after she comes, but this time she says, "I'm too excited and I don't want to miss a minute of you." Shayna runs her palm across the arc of Knaydle's belly, then slips her fingers under the lowest fold and rocks her flesh. Knaydle shudders, but can't keep from remembering what time it is.

"Honey, I can't, I have to go to the meeting—"

Shayna shakes her head, pulls Knaydle's hand to her mouth, kissing it. "And everyone thinks I'm the one who's controlled."

"I'm not controlled—but I do have a schedule. I've only got thirty minutes, and I want to put on clean clothes. Don't worry, I'll be back."

"Worried, I'm not," Shayna says, almost to herself. She changes into her jeans and the T-shirt from the Italian restaurant around the corner that says "escape responsibility" on the back, while Knaydle puts her laundry in the dryer downstairs.

Shayna warms up leftover tofu and rice. She realizes she's smiling at her rice, and puts down her fork, watching Knaydle finish eating.

"Who would know," Knaydle says, wiping her mouth, getting up to leave, "to look at you—such a nice Jewish lady, a librarian, even—what a slut you really are."

172

"Don't tell," Shayna says.

"No one?"

"No one."

"How about if I write a story about it?

"That would be okay."

"It's okay to tell everyone but not to tell anyone?"

"Exactly," Shayna says, blushing, and Knaydle pulls Shayna's hands to the curve of her cheek again, taking the time, breathless, on her way.

DINOFLAGELLATES

In the moonless, humid night a rusty school bus pitches over a sand track, swatted by palm fronds as if it were a large yellow bug. Felice holds Fanny's hand, low, against the torn brown plastic of the bench. Fanny is being a good sport about adventures in the Vieques heat, although at night the heat is greased by breeze, and this close to the coast becomes pliable, buttery. Fanny finds she can breathe in humidity, recovered now from the ten-seater plane ride from San Juan that tipped her within scraping distance of the giant bamboo groves in El Yunque, the rain forest.

As the bus inches along the hidden road, Felice and Fanny use the lurches to press their thighs together in secret pleasure. They are middle-aged, and for the six years of their alliance, traveling has increased their appetite for each other. Aside from the obvious—no phones, no routine—they thrive on visual stimulation and slightly edgy situations, moments when they must find their way and succeed. Their desire is a map with half the roads obscured by the creases that come from folding it so many times and carrying it in a back pocket. Each successful navigation is a fresh delight.

The bus rocks to a stop on a mat of beach vegetation several inches before its wheels would have stuck in the soft beach. They are the last to alight of the eighteen tourists and female tour guide. The male bus driver waits by the bus, smoking, which, he insists in Spanish, keeps the mosquitoes away. The other tourists are heterosexual couples or families, three pre-adolescent children between them. In order to get the full wonder, tours to the phosphorescent bay are recommended at the new moon, when the night is black as squid ink stippled only by the Milky Way. On this side of Vieques, away from the military base so often the site of anti-U.S. demonstrations, few lights pollute the dark. The woman who runs the tour is ecology- and nature-minded—she uses an electric engine on her boat to cut down on oil entering the water.

Felice spent part of her childhood in Puerto Rico, and over the last thirty years, she has taken several lovers to see the more famous phosphorescent bay on the main island. Even though a relatively small percentage of tourists leave the beach and casino strip around San Juan, the double-decker boats that stream out to the bay in La Parguera have been carrying too many people for too many decades. Felice's last trip there with some hundred tourists was disappointing—a few flashes as the large boat disturbed the entrance to the cove, a pail of murky water laced with faint gleaming. She'd read that the dinoflagellate population at La Parguera, the one-celled creatures that used to sparkle up the Caribbean dark, is endangered now.

So this time she altered the tour, having found a lesbian-owned guest house on Vieques. In the guest house, which straddled a volcanic hill covered with dense green vegetation, they were the only lesbians besides the owners. The hammocks had views of both the Atlantic and Caribbean seas. It was gorgeous enough but Felice, inured to the more blatant charms of the topography and restless, had spied a notice about the phosphorescent tour tacked on the bulletin board, and persuaded Fanny to give it a try.

Fanny likes being gently persuaded, lovingly cajoled into trying things she hasn't imagined. She likes to taste new things if they come vouched for, and Felice likes to vouch. They are both big—Felice too big for the life jackets that the tour guide offers, but then, she has a cold, and has been pushing herself because, after all, how many chances do you get to show your lover the sights of the tropics? Really they've come because her father died nearly a year ago; her family consented to schedule the prescribed ritual unveiling of the headstone to fit her winter break. Within a week, they must circle back and stand by the grave with Felice's mother and brothers in a rural Puerto Rican cemetery that has a small Jewish section.

Yet tonight they are gliding out on a small boat that rides low in the smooth water. The guide cuts the engine as a large shape glides by, outlined in yellow light. "That's a turtle," the guides tells them, clearly pleased. "Watch for other fish." As they adjust to the obsidian shine of the water ringed by mangrove trees, fish part the surface with electric jaws, snapping at bugs that leave footprints for bait by disturbing the microscopic florescence even with their tiny weight. *Dinoflagellate,* who wouldn't swoon to say it, roll it around in her mouth, suck at its undulation?

The guide invites her passengers to swim in the bay. Felice would never admit to being terrified of getting into opaque water, even if the creatures that lie still in the deep will flash, betraying themselves when they move to bite. Anyway, she has a cold. Anyway, the life jacket doesn't fit. Fanny has her bathing suit on under her clothes, and is swept up in Felice's encouragement. Usually it's Felice who takes the dare and dives into the cold wave or snorkels along the shallow shore, only a little concerned about scraping herself on the purple spines of sea urchins. But she can see the spines. Fanny does not know until she reads this story how glad Felice is to have the cold and life jacket problem to fall back on, so Fanny bravely, happily even, descends the ladder off the boat. Into the dark bay she goes with about ten of the other tourists, shouting, flapping, making a sudden carnival splash of color in the night, setting the dinoflagellates into panics of bio-luminescence.

Fanny hauls herself back on deck, laughing and sweeps Felice up to her dripping body. The other tourists are paying no attention to them—everyone is transfixed by the glittering that washes over the deck from the wet swimmers. Felice pulls the top of Fanny's bathing suit down and stares between her breasts. Here the constellations spark against Fanny's flesh, showing the way—between her bathing suit and body shine a thousand stars.

DEBORAH VOTES

"So where's the bus?" Mrs. Landauer complained to the man standing next to her. He shrugged, poking at a weed in the concrete with his cane.

"Always shuffling us around like the hoi polloi. I have better things to do than wait." She adjusted the strap on her shoulder bag, emanating exasperation.

Honestly, Deborah Kaplan thought, *watching the bus pull to the Adams House curb, these people don't know anything about waiting. They should be excited, delighted even, to have such efficient transportation. And today especially.*

On Mondays, Wednesdays and Fridays the bus took them to various shopping centers so the seniors could have a choice between supermarkets, drugstores and the variety of mall shops that flourished like mold in the Florida heat. But today, Tuesday, November 8, they were going to vote.

Deborah hadn't voted for President of the United States since she cast her ballot for Adlai Stevenson on Long Island some forty years before. Shortly after that, her husband, an electrical engineer, was sent by his company to Puerto Rico. "Only for a year," they promised. But when his assignment was up, Saul volunteered for a permanent position. "If Jesus Christ had started his Second Coming in Puerto Rico, he'd have given the whole thing up to enjoy paradise," Saul liked to say. Of course, he didn't have to go to the supermarket and try to find a head of lettuce that wasn't rotten, or try to run errands before the children got out of school only to find that everything was shut down from noon to two, and after that no one had the energy to accomplish anything, including Deborah. And it didn't seem to bother him that Puerto Rico didn't have electoral votes—for him, it was a good deal. No vote, no Federal taxes. But she still regretted not having been able to vote for Kennedy and against that criminal, Nixon.

Well that's certainly old business, Deborah thought, gazing over Mrs. Landauer's neatly styled white head at the flat, landscaped parcels moving by. "When people here ask if my husband's dead, I just say yes and give them a little sigh. Let them think what they want. They don't have to know we were divorced twenty-five years ago, do they?" She asked her daughter Becky this question every couple of months during a phone call, often while Deborah was watching a Cubs game with the sound muted. Her daughter did not take the repetition as a sign that Deborah was losing her memory—far from it. After all, since she'd turned 50, Becky had trouble remembering how she'd told her coming out story to a particular friend, or the name of that movie star she liked so much who quit acting and became a British politician.

"Glenda Jackson," Deborah said without hesitation. "I saw her in 'A Touch of Class' again last week—now she was a gorgeous woman. Too bad she gave up acting. Do you remember how much you liked her in 'Marat/Sade'?"

"She was fabulous, Mom," Becky replied, sorting laundry across the continent, in California. "I remember it exactly, even though I had never seen her before, and we were sitting in the balcony. But I couldn't remember her name."

"I know what you mean," Deborah said, and Becky could hear her exhaling a stream of cigarette smoke. Becky wished Deborah would give up smoking, but then every abstinent child likes her parents to embrace her chosen virtues.

Deborah considered her children extraordinary, even though she felt compelled to add that every mother thinks her children are the best and brightest—she knew a thing or two about the evil eye. One of the women at Adams House liked to gloat about her son the Congressman, but Deborah suspected he'd bought the seat with stock market money. What ever happened to grass roots politicians? Well, she didn't want to speak ill of him—she didn't even know him. And she was genuinely glad his mother had occasion for pride.

Three years ago, Becky and her brother Jason met Deborah in Fort Lauderdale and commenced a tour of twelve retirement communities. Who knew places like Adams House even existed? As far as she knew, they didn't have any in Puerto Rico. But with Saul dead and buried in a manicured plot out in Caguas, and that whore he married looking after his grave, Deborah was free to do as she pleased. She retired from her job as a children's librarian with a little money saved, social security and a small inheritance from her mother. 1996 was a particularly bad hurricane season, and although the island wasn't devastated as it had been during Hugo, every heavy wind brought new power outages.

Sometimes the power would be out for as long as five days, even on the hotel strip where Deborah lived, and Deborah's apartment was two flights up. She had trouble with her legs, and the sewage system sprung leaks every three or four months in the basement parking lot, eventually ruining the finish on her car. For what, she wanted to know, did she need the aggravation of owning a car and an apartment? She'd miss being able to walk a block to the blackjack tables, but enough is enough. She determined to sell that apartment before the mildew and termites destroyed it, and move back to the States.

She tried out November at her daughter's place in California, and went to visit her Brooklyn grandchildren for a February birthday. But forty years in the tropics had stamped her—she could no longer bear the cold. No promise of central heating and indoor pools could dissuade her from picking Florida, though god knows she claimed for years that she'd never live in Florida.

"Florida?" Her sophisticated children and sisters were horrified. Florida was where bubbes went, yentas with thick accents, to live in segregated groups away from people of color and the white southerners who still despised Jews.

When Deborah visited Becky in Oakland, she suspected her family had conspired to get her to reconsider. Becky took to her to the fancy restaurant in St. Helena that Deborah liked—the one with the fountain in the form of a sculpture of a wire table, complete with bread and perpetually spilling wine. Friends of Becky's who lived in the country joined them.

"My mother's lived in Florida for the last fifteen years," one of the friends confided to Deborah over wild mushrooms on seared polenta with duck reduction appetizer, "and I don't know if a progressive woman like yourself will be comfortable there—so many of the white people, even the Jews, are extremely conservative."

"I'm an adaptable person, aren't I?" Deborah asked Becky and Jason as they shlepped through the twelve arts and crafts rooms of the retirement communities on Jason's list. "I've learned to hold my tongue." Becky and Jason exchanged a glance, remembering the mother who'd staged her own sit-ins in airports over lost reservations; who, when she found out about their father's affair, railed bitterly against him until his death.

But Deborah's self-evaluation was correct—she enjoyed people ("Up to a point," she liked to say) and always had plenty to talk about without engaging in politics or religion; and she was relatively diplomatic in conveying that she would not abide derogatory remarks about any group. After five days of polite sales managers—all of whom wore a variation on the circle pin, as if they were members of a secret society—Deborah chose a place that had a nice outdoor pool, her favorite baseball cable channel, and featured "a nice mix of Jewish and gentile residents," as the sales agent put it. She rejected the facility run by the Grossinger family, even though they had a Workman's Circle discussion group. "Doesn't it strike you as ironic to organize for social justice in a gated community?" she wanted to know. Her children agreed.

Deborah liked the Adams House bus drivers, and spoke Spanish with those who were Latino. They smiled at her odd accent, but were impressed by both her fluency and desire to engage them. Sometimes she felt more at ease with the staff than the other residents, whose favorite topic of conversation was their portfolios. *Even without gates, Florida's a segregated place,* she thought, as they pulled up in front of the elementary school that provided their polling place. The only African American person around was their bus driver.

She'd already voted in a Congressional election; the ballots were completely different from San Juan, so she got help the first time. She prepared carefully for her second election, studying the sample ballot. Now she brought one into the voting booth with her, pulling it out of the large white purse she always carried. The Brandeis alumni women's group held voter education debates at Adams House, and Deborah was among the handful of residents who took the opportunity to attend.

"They give us so many choices here," she told Becky, "yet most of the residents complain there's nothing to do, and wait for bingo night."

"It's a poor second to blackjack," Becky said.

Deborah laughed.

In the voting booth, she took a minute to orient herself, and sighed with pleasure before she opened the ballot. It was good they put the names in big type, but interlocking the candidates on both sides of the page—that was odd. She adjusted her reading glasses. Her hand wavered for a minute, as she tried to decide which hole to punch for Al Gore.

"If you vote for that shmendrick Nader—did you see what his position on abortion is?" she had demanded of Becky.

"I agree that Nader is a jerk about women, Mom." Becky was a little guilty about this evasion, since she planned to vote for the Green Party, with which she was registered. She was fond of Winona LaDuke, the first Native American woman to run for Vice President, but the real point was to get people besides Democrats and Republicans taken seriously. Besides, she hadn't ever voted for a man who had won the White House, and thought it might jinx Gore if she switched her allegiance now. California was clearly going to the Democrats—she e-mailed all these reasons to her brother, but never told her mother.

When Deborah lived in Puerto Rico, she and Becky rarely talked on the phone—only on birthdays, special occasions or for emergencies. Although by the 1990's it was often cheaper to call San Juan than New York, both of them cleaved to their old perception of the enormous expense and difficulty of making a long distance connection via cable that lay buried under the Atlantic. They remembered phone calls from thirty years ago full of echoes, the sound of the lost souls in the Bermuda Triangle bouncing through the lines. Now they talked once a week, on Sunday mornings, Pacific time, an hour before Becky went swimming and right after Deborah had lunch. "I do miss you more here," Deborah confessed. "It's an artificial environment, after all."

Becky had been hoping Deborah wouldn't notice. The idea of a central building with independent apartments and shared transportation, in its pure form, sounded like the kind of communal living space Becky had envisioned as a revolutionary ideal when she was young, and had never really given up on. Pastel barracks transformed by hotel chains into profit centers with cheerful social directors shepherding old folks to bingo games was a depressing readjustment of vision, but she had wanted to believe that straight people would not find it as alienating as she, a lesbian, would. Perhaps that was true, but it didn't mean they—her mother—couldn't see the sterility and forced congeniality that "getting along" required.

Still, Deborah Kaplan made the best of it. She found women who liked having her as a regular dinner companion—one who would lend her car when necessary (although she didn't like to borrow or impose), and another who would go to duplicate bridge games on Saturday afternoons. Deborah was a Life Master at the Platinum level, quite an accomplishment for someone who lived in Puerto Rico and rarely could afford going to major tournaments, as she took pleasure in reminding her family. But she didn't brag to her neighbors in the retirement community, and if they roped her into sitting in on one of their amateur games, she did her best to be amused and generous. She declined these offers as often as she could, though, because stupidity of any kind rankled her.

It had been hard to keep her equanimity in the face of the campaign—Gore was no prize, but that man, Bush, and his father's cronies—how could anyone take him seriously? *The New York Times* did a whole exposé about how he barely worked as governor, and her ten-year-old grandson had a better vocabulary. America would be the laughing stock of the world if he got elected.

"You remember Joanne, my dinner partner? She takes everything so personally, honestly. I had to stop talking about the election because she was quaking in terror through every meal."

"She can't just disagree with you?"

"Not like my other dinner partner, Nancy. We didn't agree on a thing, not a thing, but we had fun. She called me a northern liberal, even though she came from Vermont. But she didn't take everything to heart the way Joanne does. I do miss Nancy." The other part about living at Adams House, the part Deborah hadn't been prepared for, was how often someone you've recently developed an affection for dropped dead.

"It's better if you can enjoy the argument," Becky said.

"Exactly." Deborah sucked at her cigarette. "But I can't upset Joanne, so I have to watch what I say around her. The Catholic Church says she has to vote for Bush, because he's anti-abortion, so she's going to. Can you imagine?"

"She's going to do what the church tells her?"

"Don't be naive, dear. Millions of people do."

"Sorry to sound naive, Mom. I really did know that."

"Of course you did. Speaking of which, you know what they put on the lecture schedule for next month?"

"What?" Becky was packing her gym bag to go swimming, grateful for portable phones.

"They're bringing in a priest to talk about the connection between Chanukah and Christmas. It just galls me. I told Joanne at dinner that there is no connection, certainly not enough for a priest to give a lecture on. It's ludicrous. I told her it would be like giving a lecture on the connection between Ramadan and Christmas. You know what she said to me?"

"'What's Ramadan?'?" Becky was listening, despite her divided attention.

"Exactly. You are clever. 'What's Ramadan?' I tell you. I am fond of Joanne, but she's led such a sheltered life. Sometimes I think I scare her half to death."

"Well, try not to give her a heart attack. The election should be angst enough."

"You are going to vote on Tuesday?"

"Of course, Mom—I always vote." Becky remembered the postcard she'd seen, stuck on someone's refrigerator—"If voting changed anything, they'd make it illegal." It always surprised her how seriously she took it anyway.

Becky called her mother Wednesday night, although she had hardly slept. She'd had the unpleasant sensation of channeling Al Gore's misery, wondering how in hell he'd managed to lose the Democratic stronghold of Ohio.

"Your mother was on the news," Deborah said.

"You were?"

"I tell you, I vote for the first time in forty years, and it has to be in the butterfly ballot county. I told them you could have all your faculties and still find it confusing."

"Did you get a tape of it?"

"Oh, I didn't think of that. I'm not as technological as you children."

"It's okay, Mom."

"But you're right, I would have liked for you to see it. I got one of the drivers to take me down to the local Democratic campaign office so I could tell them my story, how many of the retirees here still aren't sure whom they voted for, and you know many of them are as sharp as I am."

"It's not a question of sharp, Mom."

"That's exactly what I said. Some young reporter—younger than you—picked me out. You'd have been proud of me—I was very well-spoken."

"I'm sure you were."

"I mean, they had a man on the news, and he said, 'I am a rocket scientist, and I found it confusing.' A rocket scientist!" Deborah snorted.

"It's terrible, Mom," Becky said, and kept saying, as they commiserated about the sorry state of the country every week.

"I'm keeping a file on this—I've got all the clippings about every irregularity. It's in my bottom file drawer, next to the wills. Don't you dare throw it out."

"Of course not," Becky said, refraining from telling Deborah that the Internet probably archived all those articles. Of course, as she told her students, the Internet can be sabotaged, the electron building blocks of data rearranged. Perhaps her mother's files would turn out to be important someday.

"They ask me why I'm so upset, after all these months. Why I can't be gracious about the loss. I never thought I'd end up with so many Republicans—and so many people who could care less," Deborah said in February.

"Florida is not the most liberal place in the world." Becky considered how soon she could schedule time for her next visit.

"I knew that. But this! They'd be upset if they lost a diamond bracelet—that's what's important to them. Well, I tell them, if I could afford a diamond bracelet, then I could afford to replace it. It's only a thing. But democracy! If you lose democracy—."

REBECCA'S GARDEN

The October light was crisp around its edge, and even though the air was warm, underneath was the cool promise of a mother's lips on your forehead, kissing to check for fever. With the top down on her nearly-new convertible, Felice lifted her face up to feel that kiss as she whipped over the San Rafael bridge, gratified to be going against the traffic. *Sweet luck, don't leave me yet,* she thought, amused with herself, pulling up in front of her friend Rebecca's. Near the finish of her next-to-last menstrual cycle, Felice was invited to pull up a folding chair at the end of Rebecca's driveway and survey the garden. The dried corn stalks stood in a line six feet long, a frayed hedge, spiky husks of growth that Rebecca did not know what to do with. "I could put them in one of those noisy shredders, but I hate it when other people do that," she told Felice.

Rebecca had become increasingly sensitive to the world since they had been young printers twenty-some years before, putting out pamphlets in secret after the press closed—now she was prone to seizures that could be caused by any loud noise or strong scent. Consequently, it had been many years since she drove. Felice only saw Rebecca when she slowed down enough to miss her friend and make a date bounded on both ends by rush hour; or when Rebecca needed refuge at Felice's home in Oakland, which Felice tried to keep relatively environmentally safe—safer than Rebecca's neighbors fumigating or replacing a roof and raising pillars of dust. Every couple years, they might also meet in Berkeley when one of Rebecca's attendants took her for errands and visits.

In today's flannel October breeze, Felice squirmed in the camp chair Rebecca had provided, realizing how her relatively easy access to a life of highways fueled her inattention. *Shouldn't she be listening?* What Rebecca liked best in her garden were "the brussels sprout trees," as she called them, their odd stems studded with green beads and topped with a crown of large, tropical leaves. They discussed the taste of brussels sprouts, which Rebecca said were supposed to be superior if eaten minutes off the stalk, popped from your gathering hand into hot water, and then into your mouth. But Rebecca allowed she didn't quite like the taste of brussels sprouts, and didn't know if the rumor about fresh taste was true, since this was her first year growing them. What Rebecca really liked was looking at them grow.

Felice surveyed the garden and noticed that the far wall was frothing with purple-blue morning glories, growing up over the wide leaves of a grape vine. The blossoms were much larger than the ones inching up a trellis in her own backyard—in fact, the morning glories at home were about done for the season. She figured this because her lover had been playing with the seedpods, dumping them into the dirt of the bucket in which they were planted. Here in Rebecca's yard, the morning glories had taken off, and they were flowing upward like a waterspout through a wide, green stand of bamboo—a purple plume muscling into the sky.

"What's the word I want for that?" Rebecca said. She paused, trying to avoid the word gardeners use for weeds, invasive. They both considered the vine. "Enthusiastic—that's it. The morning glories are enthusiastic."

"If I painted, I would paint that," Felice said, meaning it, wishing she could paint and remembering that once, more than thirty-five years ago, she'd had canvases and played with the swirling oil, trying to express a very particular emotion—the emotion of a thirteen-year-old girl locked up for trying to commit suicide. Suicidal impulses were long behind her now. She wanted to believe that the spirit of Georgia O'Keeffe would inhabit her hands if she went to the art store on the way home, and help her render the way she saw the brightness of the morning glories cutting through the ordinary green of the place they lived. Is there such a thing as ordinary green? When her father was alive, he liked to talk of artists going to the tropics in search of every green variant. Behind the morning glories, then, gleamed a self-conscious hipster green that secretly prepared for drought, blowing a few cool notes to highlight the delicacy of the purplish rush toward the season's diminishing light. *Could she paint the essence of things as they entered consciousness through shape, color, smell, sensation? Could anyone? Were they all disgusted in the end with how representation never came close to experience? Was that why art had turned to abstraction?*

"For instance," Felice asked at lunch, "how do you convey the feel of wind in paint, or in words for that matter?" She and Rebecca had been discussing the nature of the wind, since a powerful one had been raking the bay for the last thirty hours, and was only now settling down to a manageable breeze. At home, Felice's street was filled with branches, leaves, debris, and the power had gone out for awhile the night before.

Rebecca shook her head as if she found the question funny. "How do you convey the soul in poetry?"

Felice and Rebecca had been friends for more or less fifteen years; they had an old conversation about the nature of the soul between them, an investigation that they once carried on over the din of offset presses, into what it would mean for the soul to be divisible, presuming that souls exist. Is all soul one soul? Then it must be divisible, since we each have a part. But if it's not, our isolation is complete and eternal—that was the nature of their debate, for the sake of which they had switched sides on and off over the years, always coming back to it with new images and considerations.

"Is the wind divisible?" Felice asked, and Rebecca laughed out loud.

"Well, phenomena like the Santa Ana winds are distinct patterns—did you ever live in L.A.?"

"Not long enough to notice repetition," Felice said.

"Those patterns might seem to have a relationship to what humans do—some kind of payback for changing the environment," Rebecca said. "But I think they exist apart from humans, and just affect our behavior. Like Van Gogh's compulsion to go into the huge winds of the mistral, tying himself to the easel to paint and having seizures afterward. And the khamsin in the Sahara—if there's a khamsin, crimes of passion can be legally excused. These winds are particular to places and have names. So aren't they different in some substantial way from the average wind that comes from the ocean?"

"But think of the wind as skin—"

"As skin? I think of the ground, the dirt, as the Earth's skin. The wind could be its aura maybe. I don't think that analogy is viable."

"But if the Earth is a body, the world could be the organs, and the wind stretching out and covering everything—" Felice paused, searching for words.

"Would you call lips skin?" Rebecca asked.

"Yes—a kind of skin."

"Well," Rebecca said, touching her lips, "that's a difference in geography. Maybe it makes sense."

"Right—because even in the body—even if the body is healthy—you can get a boil somewhere—like a hurricane."

Rebecca slowly ate the beets and polenta she'd ordered, considering. "You could look at it that way."

"And besides, the world isn't healthy. When I was coming back from Florida last month, we took off into the sunset, so we got that long extended twilight that lasts for hours." Felice gestured to indicate the horizon. "And it's very pretty at its edge, but underneath the air looked like somebody'd taken a shit in it that had diffused over the whole planet. Finally I decided the air looked so awful because it was evening, and darkening under the clouds, but still, it didn't look right."

This was what Felice meant about painting—in her mind, O'Keeffe's paintings of clouds were what clouds looked like—and when she looked out of the airplane and the clouds arranged themselves in ways that recalled the cloud paintings, she realized she had substituted the image for the experience in her mind. Nevertheless, the thing you couldn't put in a painting was still the air—the wind feathery against their bodies when they sat in Rebecca's garden looking at the morning glories or the stale air in an airplane cabin, full of coughs, sighs and shallow breaths.

Rebecca wouldn't let Felice pay the bill for lunch, although Felice, who had inherited enough to speculate in the stock market they once hexed, would have felt more comfortable springing for it every time. "Since I don't have attendants right now, I have all this attendant money," Rebecca explained. But she needed a few singles for the tip, and Felice had a couple of the new dollar coins, which she put down.

"Who is this?" Rebecca turned the brassy-gold coin over and squinted at the engraving.

"Sacagewea," Felice said.

"It doesn't look like the pictures I've seen of her."

"It's very homogenized," Felice said, shorthand for *what do you expect—they couldn't even bother to put her name on it.*

193

"I recently read a book that made the Trail of Tears real to me—I mean, I had always glossed over it, Trail of Tears, but I hadn't thought—felt—what it would be like, every day," Rebecca said.

Felice looked away into the place where humans suffer, where armies take advantage of their power to promote an ethic of cruelty. She didn't want to think about it too closely, either. The cold, the people dying, the smell. The government of her own country did this thing that is mostly forgotten, which she herself had forgotten.

Rebecca went into some detail about the book; the main character, a woman, surviving partially through her alliance with a white soldier and the problems that alliance causes with her husband, her community. "*Pushing the Bear,* which is the metaphor for death—it works. The woman who wrote it is also mixed blood," she said. Rebecca's father was Native American, her mother Jewish, although they had both conspired to appear neutral in the Midwest cities where they'd lived, passing as another Protestant couple.

"Early in the book, the woman gets to go back to her house for a cooking pot and blanket—the soldier takes her—but when she gets there, white people have already moved in." By this time, they had loaded Rebecca's portable oxygen tank in Felice's car and were heading back to her garden. "The parallels with the Jews in Germany are very intense—she was so upset by how her things had been mixed in with the white people's but put in the wrong places, used for the wrong reasons, she could barely remember why she'd come. Remember, the Cherokees were one of the 'five civilized tribes' and whites thought what they had—not only their land but their houses, their stuff—was worth having. Can you imagine how that must feel—to have your altar cauldron, for instance, used as a chamber pot?"

194

As a Jew, Felice thought she could imagine it. She wanted to say something about American arrogance, but she was anxious that she not presume on Rebecca's life; that is, that she not presume they were the same in this. The Trail of Tears, the broken treaties—she could say her ancestors were being dragged, burned, raped in Eastern Europe while that was happening—but this week her relations, if you kept on in that blood-line association, were killing Palestinians. *The sovereign power of an individual to refuse sovereign powers—does that make any sense at all? Does it help?* Still, Felice wanted to make common cause because she felt close to Rebecca, because she understood how moments in history can scrape their nails along your flesh, drawing blood.

"When I was on tour in Germany this summer," Felice said, "I really felt how Germans' lives are shaped by an absence they don't talk about. It made me realize how that absence shapes our lives here—what we don't acknowledge, the genocidal war America fought—is still fighting."

They had the top down on Felice's convertible—whatever Rebecca said, and she said something, was lost in the noisy air.

When they got back, Rebecca showed Felice the blooms of her passion flower—the incredible wavy white petals, a stiff fringe circling a more traditional core—explaining how difficult it was to transplant it, how it almost didn't survive, how she'd had to root out the morning glories from that spot so the passion flower might stretch and take hold. They toured the plants still fruiting—carrot tops shouldering through basil, the chard, which was called an annual on the seed package, that had been going for two years. "It just won't stop," Rebecca said. "'Let me give a little more, and a little more,' it says." Then she gave Felice a large red curving Anaheim pepper, "Too hot for me now." And they sat, discussing the brussels sprouts, the tomatoes, the grapes gone by, what kind of gardening sensibilities could be hoped for when new neighbors moved in.

Could she keep the afternoon? Had she been present at all? Why did she resist making these dates when it was such an easy pleasure to talk and look at plants? Walking towards her car Felice noticed a tree in front of Rebecca's apartment, a liquid amber gum that was beginning to turn—in California, trees turn so late, late October to late November, that it seems as if Fall doesn't really come. But now that she has a convertible she looks up more, and notices that many trees here turn, in small patches, sometimes three or four on a street at once, or at least partly at once. The world blazes and then fades, but it's still possible to catch the blazing moments in your mind. The corn stalks dry up and become a problem of disposal, the big heads of dried sunflowers droop to the ground, doubling their spindly stems.

With only a few pushes of buttons, she had the top down again, and was heading out into the wind, across the Richmond Bridge.

RIDER

The rain makes a curtain, a haze, a buzz, a fluttering, a mist and the frogs, encouraged to think the whole world has become pond, fling themselves forward and are shocked by the insult of pavement as headlights swing out through the dark—for one, a near miss, for the next, quick death.

Felice wonders who will know this, who will write this story—a fifty-one year old woman pushes the big wooden gates of the artists' retreat open and wiggles the black convertible, the low-slung, rain-spiffed sports car, onto the hilly road, trying to gauge how far to "Queer Casino Night" in Lincoln City. When she locks the gate, she checks the map. *Damn, too far.* She'd thought Lincoln City was a quarter inch below Tillamook, but it's forty miles below, and Tillamook—she remembers the signs—is twenty something past Wheeler, which is twelve miles from these gates.

Nevertheless, she starts south. It's beginning to get dark. Her mind is big, restless, confronting itself with the constant news that time is all one thing, she has been here before, a wide wing flicking the western coast of the United States of America, strut-ting her axles through small towns with one or three bars open after eight, and then miles of cliff edge punctuated by rivers and road, the road always about to cave in, wash out—and will, some year, be gone when human life sputters to its close, a few last refugees walking delicately past old asphalt bones, hoping to find a horde of surviving salmon. If only she had a joint. She aches to smoke, to burn her lungs that pump the fir-cleaned air into the fine spurts of blood moving around through her more or less *healthy—healthy?—oh, what the hell, imagine it's healthy—* body. Healthy enough tonight, though her eyesight isn't as good as it should be—a car's taillights, 300, 500 feet ahead, tremble and blur. But the road signs, as she comes up to them, are clear.

Past Wheeler, she looks down and registers only a quarter of a tank. How far can she go without finding an open gas station before it's too late to turn back? This edgy thought makes her sharp, and the sharpness is a hard pleasure in the deepening night along the almost empty stretches of Route 101 going south. No gas at all in Wheeler, and as she comes up to Rockaway Beach, no stations open either, despite that it's a tourist town with at least three restaurants—a Mexican place, a pizza parlor, a pig and pancake diner, and now a cafe, a closed espresso joint on the far edge. Many years ago she and T. stayed in a motel in Rockaway—*no, don't remember that time T. wanted to make love and you wouldn't give in to being soothed, wouldn't smooth over T's regular brutality. Rewind,* she thinks, *or, at least, overlap the time lapse photo track of that relationship.* She sighs as she succeeds.

Time lapse itself is what she gets—the red streaks that cars leave in a picture of Times Square in *Life Magazine,* circa 1958. Driving up Route 5 six years ago to visit Oregon friends, she stopped on a hill outside Roseburg and bumped into her half-life image, Felice and K. arguing about whether to go to the women's Seder in Eugene. "No," Felice had said or was saying, "they try to reinvent what's tainted as if childhood could be reframed in a ritual with the words changed. Let's go home." And they did. She reaches out to tell herself how many Seders she's gone to since and survived. *Ease up, kid.* But that other, stranded self refuses to hear.

Felice laughs out loud, curves with the pavement's sway, the motion of sand dunes imposed on the arc of road. Somewhere near Canon Beach, she and S. were taking a trail, the first trip together up the coast, twelve years ago already, when Felice was giving S. the tour of West Coast wonders. She'd had to shit suddenly, and couldn't reach to wipe herself while squatting in the woods. S. wiped her butt. Does S. remember that now? Her shame, S.'s matter of fact ease, kindness, generosity? This isn't what she meant to tell. *Not love, but time that binds and time is all in the mind.* She taps *mind mind mind* on the steering wheel, trying to catch the rhythm of water splattering on the windshield. Just a big old dyke intent, intense, fiddling with the wiper speeds, jamming through water-logged March.

In Garibaldi they had crab races last week, which Felice found by accident Saturday afternoon, following signs to a rec hall by the harbor. People pulled crabs out of tanks, waiting to see which angry claw would scoot down its track first, then threw the crabs back in tanks to race again with new numbers. The lucky winners, not the crabs but the human registrants, won prizes and crab dinners. *What isolated white folks won't do to amuse themselves in rainy season,* Felice thought. Thank god, goddess, whatever, the Garibaldi Texaco station is open, and since it's Oregon, which has a law against self-service, the boy has to stop talking to his girlfriend who's sitting there in her parents' car, and fill the tank. He tops it off, the way guys usually do in these small town stations, squeezing nickels out of nozzles. Felice watches carefully to see he's not so distracted as to forget the gas cap.

Relaxed now, still thrumming, she passes a place she read about that's supposed to be good for dinner, a cafe in an art gallery, but she wants to see how she feels when she gets to Tillamook, if she's going to keep on to casino night. Tillamook is a strip mall, a cheese factory, and something else—paper mill or refinery out on a spit, a flame encased in fog above orange lights in case some errant prop plane might find itself too close.

Felice sweeps the sky for a pilot, who would have to have a thought as tight and alone as hers to go up in the night, merely to burn fossil fuel and listen to the radio, some public station with a scratchy history of migrant worker blues punctuated with folk tunes, stories about riots and Pinkertons and Wobblies, all of which are familiar as jazz, half remembered. On the radio wave she's riding, her radical actions, "two/four/six/eight dykes are gonna smash the state," are joined to this woman so comfortable in her stock market bought car, when the stock market was good. A guy on the radio sings about the luxuries of the rich being bought with his blood, and the narrator tells a story of a boy killed by agricultural poisons who becomes a ghost vandal.

She drives all the way through Tillamook and then decides, *that's enough.* Turns left into a dirt lot, checks the map to see it's a good forty miles left to Lincoln City, and for what? To watch some closet queens dance to old Donna Summer tapes and lose a hundred bucks playing blackjack, if they even use real money on casino night, while she pretends not to know that migrant workers are still abused in this, in every state? Cranberries, grass seed, apples come from Oregon. She turns back. It's ten to eight when she gets to the Bay City restaurant, walks in through the art gallery, very nice, but the women in the kitchen insist they're almost done cleaning up, not serving dinner any more. At ten to eight? Saturday night? They shrug. It's March, two tables are finishing. *Well. Big deal.* The most Felice can be is hungry, the longest it can be is an hour back to the gate if she doesn't skid on a damn frog and land somewhere in 1979.

The women in the restaurant suggest the Pirate's Cove if it's open, and she goes on. The places with lights in Garibaldi are all bars, or restaurants with no one at the tables except the cook talking to somebody—you have to drive slow through Oregon coastal towns or the cops will get you, slow enough to see the life that goes on inside, if there is any. Rockaway's the same, even the Pig and Pancake House, which says "Open" but has no cars in front. The pizza place, The Rock, has cars, and when she pulls up to the door, Felice sees it's actually open till ten on Saturday night, servicing the motels with takeout. Inside she orders a clam and garlic pizza since what she really wants is seafood, why else go out to eat on the Oregon coast? The pizza is almost edible, but the clams are what anyone can get out of a can. Felice and K. used to joke about pizza on the coast, how it was like eating tenderized Frisbees covered in grease. Now, two hundred miles north of where they once lived, or live still, she isn't entirely clear, she bites into the over-yeasted crust.

Coming north three weeks ago, she slowed by the gravel inlet off the main road where she and K. had their Oregon home, and in 1982 in a steady drizzle, buried her dog Grindle under a wide hemlock tree. The hole they dug was deep, waist high; K. stood and held her shovel up while Felice observed a small rainbow over the blackberry bushes that lined the yard. *That's too corny,* she thought, *whether or not anyone believes it.* Grindle ran orange and tan on the soft fur ground of redwood forest, was patient on long road trips, loyal and regal in the studio while Felice worked. Driving up this time, Felice caught sight of a flag with a golden retriever appliqué as she drove by the signpost for her old road. She squeaked a wide U-turn and made a left past the thicket of uva ursi where rabbits hid, drove up to the aluminum fence, and eight golden retrievers flounced down the yard to greet her. The man who bred them did not seem impressed she had planted a dog there, and the same kind had sprung up and multiplied. He wanted to talk about his new shed, and she listened.

You still can't get decent pizza in that town or anywhere in Oregon, except maybe Portland where wood-fired Tuscan ovens have migrated from California, but in Rockaway, clam pizza's dinner, better than disturbing her fellow resident with noise back at the retreat. While she's eating, someone says something about Jews which makes her put down the newspaper, but she can only catch their last sentence—"Well, Michael Douglas is one—." She thinks this is said with approval, is not sure. She notices one of the young men who walks out is black—not, she thinks, among those at the table talking about Jews, because it was a woman's voice— and he's the third, no fourth black male she's seen on the coast, counting the child she saw yesterday with a white woman in the health food store and a teenager at the crab races in Garibaldi. No black women. She never overhears anyone talking about African Americans or Native Americans, only Jews, though she is listening to what everyone says, listening through the curves to the sinews vibrating in their throats as they speak. She did enjoy eavesdropping on a long conversation a woman at a bar was having about someone's beautiful marijuana plants the first time Felice went into the San Dune in Manzanita for fried oysters.

Is she still healthy after what she eats? It would be great to have a cigarette, to ride all night up and down the coast listening to the radio and her CDs, smoking, burning up the night, forgetting which year this was—no, knowing which year all the years were at once, flying them in the air like her friend the juggler gets flaring torches up, the years licking at each other's flames while she plays chicken with frogs.

The rest is anti-climax, even the game of Ms. Pac-Man she plays for old time's sake, which is now, right? And Ollie's is still jumping on Telegraph Ave. with dykes hustling the pool tables and video machines, a dyke joint, not mob-owned, before its leatherette doors cracked and closed. It's easy coming back into Wheeler, so easy she drifts into wishing she'd sold her Cisco stock a year ago at 80 without fear of the tax consequences instead of holding it and now it's at 15, which she never would have guessed.

She hates thinking about the stock market, it's worse than pinball, nothing like as honest as sex or anger, the angry dreams she's been having because—this morning it came to her, waking up—she's bound up with angry women in an angry time, her work is about sticking her fingers into their fine miseries, the desire that tormented and distorted their lives, all that cleaving, splitting asunder, trying to draw closer. Better to think about them, the rhythm of their speech, the things they hoped, the colors of their ambitions, translucent, opaque.

She admires the long legs of a quick frog and then is back at the gate, pulling her blue jean jacket over turtleneck to fumble with the lock in the rain, which had been sheeting only ten minutes before. Now it's a light, sweet crude rain-oil wandering off the Pacific ledge, soaking the ground, making her storm drain rumble and drip through the night.

LEARNING TO READ

September 13, 2001 was the scheduled date for the literacy tutors' training in San Leandro, California. The organizers of the independent after-school program decided to hold it anyway—the volunteers had called in, wanting to know if the attack on the World Trade Center Towers was going to postpone their working with first and second grade girls. As it turned out, the volunteers were more eager than usual, their individual motivations pushed by public events.

At the training meeting, instructed to make introductions, Felice told the woman seated to her right that, when she wasn't volunteering, she was trying to write a novel about the Second Wave.

"Of what?" the woman asked.

"Of the women's movement," Felice answered, suspecting that the woman, a well-dressed white woman somewhere in the vicinity of her own middle-age, was baiting her.

"Do you think that feminism is dead?" the woman asked, with sincerity. It was a sincere room—volunteering to work with children is the kind of gesture that makes you feel you're contributing to a vision of a better future, even though the smoking ruins of the Twin Towers were less than forty-eight hours old. Twelve of the seventeen women at the training were doing it as their Junior League project. Felice had never knowingly seen a member of the Junior League except on TV. The well-dressed woman to her right, though, was not in their group, but was volunteering for reasons of her own. Before Felice had a chance to say anything about feminism, the meeting started.

"Write down five things that held you back as a girl and talk about them in groups of three," a very earnest young woman instructed, then collected their responses. She moved on to pre-printed pages and her rap about the organization's mission to build both skills and self-esteem. She talked about girls needing safe space and encouragement to take risks. Felice meant to tell the woman to her right that this is what happened to feminism—it didn't die. It took root. Everywhere women who had managed to gain material security were trying to give a hand up to the others. This was an easy way—working with six and seven year olds. A lot easier than a community of grown lesbians trying to share their resources, which was the kind of political work that Felice usually went in for. But encouraging girls to read—certainly a form of feminism.

Not that Felice liked to call herself a feminist, though usually it was easier than explaining why she was not. She was of course for civil and equal rights, equal pay and access. Many years ago, she had been among the organizers of a national socialist feminist convention, but when she realized she was the only one who didn't think men could be feminists, she resigned. Not from the convention, which was at that point about to begin—Felice was a responsible type, and would never leave in the middle of an action or event. Instead she resigned from feminism—and from socialism while she was at it. The first hard lesson was that ideological words got in the way of good ideas.

Two weeks later, the day she was supposed to begin her assignment at the Oakland school closest to her home, her country started bombing Afghanistan. "The bombing is great for the U.S. and for baseball," a male fan at the A's stadium actually said on the radio while she was parked outside the elementary school.

"We're too great a country to be pushed around," said a female fan. On the Internet, Felice got messages documenting the eight million people the United States has killed, or caused to be killed, since the end of WWII by its support for murderous regimes. The woman who comes from El Salvador and cleans her house every third Monday, told her that the Spanish news was reporting 3,000 dead from the air strikes. Felice, whose Spanish was more geared to restaurants than to war, was not sure she had the facts straight. "We had five and they have three already?" she asked.

"Seguro que si," the woman who cleans said. The U.S. press was reporting twenty dead.

In the bathroom, she lowered her head to her chest and heard the sound of bombers, although she knew they were planes from the airport down the road. "Everything's going to be alright in America. Let's get on with it!" is what they said on the radio. Now that she knew the name of the city Jalalabad, a beautiful name to say, to put your mouth around, she could imagine women in that city holding each other in fear, children listening to the whistling sound a bomb makes.

She'd been hearing that metallic whistle ever since she caught the second of the World Trade Towers collapsing. "Oh my god," she said, like everyone else who was watching, although she didn't believe in god. As the people she saw dying three thousand miles away groaned into the howl of girders snapping, she closed her eyes and saw the bombs poised to drop, knew that people—mostly likely people of color, in another country, would be forced to pay. She could feel the pleasure of men in war rooms, their bodies stiff with adrenaline, who would need no excuse now to explode their weapons.

She used to go to political meetings. Someone would call someone else racist or classist—and that person would turn inside out trying to show how it was not true, not true of her, she who was working towards a better world. "Defensive," the therapists called it. Folks she knew had developed a small process, in which everyone acknowledged as a matter of course that they were racist, classist, ageist, disablist—how could they not be? That way you can take responsibility for specific actions without feeling a generalized blame. But now her nation was on the defensive. And the men in power certainly didn't have the world view—the world underview—the commitment to process—that the women had in the meetings she used to attend.

The women she knew talked among themselves, went to rallies and marches, wrote letters and had been for the last four weeks; had been since the illegitimate president ascended to power. Of course, they already knew about the Taliban, knew about what happened to Moslem women under its rule. All of them agreed that terrorism was a male culture, and a horrific way to get your point across. Most of them felt that now the United States had joined the world in experiencing this loss of ordinary people caught unaware by violent death. They believed their own government to be engaged in forms of terrorism around the globe, and were frightened by its new rhetoric. Frightened for themselves and frightened for the others who were now targets. The Taliban was an evil that they hoped would be fought by the people in that region of the world. But when it came to light that the U.S. had sent the Taliban money, had trained many of its leaders in the war against the Soviets, everything became hopeless.

The United States would bomb a poor country of oppressed people and some of the Taliban would die, and someone else might come to power and everyone would still hate the United States, and the misery of the women would be compounded and new baby terrorists would vow revenge. Felice would eventually take two seven-year-olds out on the concrete playground of their school and instruct them to apologize to each other for their shoving match. "Look in each other's eyes, say what you did, and then say you're sorry." Grudgingly the girls would do this. "Try to remember to talk before you hit—we can solve almost anything with words," Felice would say to the girls. Some girls would grow up to be lesbians, yelling at each other in meetings, Afghani and Palestinian and Israeli lesbians, but finally coming to agree that if only they had the chance, they could find a way out.

The elementary school in East Oakland at which she was to help a girl learn to read sat in its own debris. Felice never understood why that section of town was called East Oakland—it was west and south of almost every other point in the city, except the Coliseum, the airport, and the Bay itself. Felice lived in a pleasant lower middle class neighborhood on the side of a hill, three blocks west of a freeway. Her street had a variety of trees—redwood, magnolia, spruce, oak, gum—and no sidewalks. She had to drive west, down 73rd Street, past the nearly empty mall, only two miles, to get to the school.

In order to volunteer, she'd had to be fingerprinted in the city of San Leandro, the first city south of Oakland, where the organization arranged for free screening with its hometown police. Felice had never voluntarily walked into a police station, but she understood the liabilities that child molesters created. Would her fingerprints turn up her shoplifting arrest twenty years ago in Idaho? Had she been fingerprinted at the Chicopee jailhouse, when her women's group was carted off for blocking the gates to the Air Force base during the Vietnam War?

The woman doing the fingerprinting used a large computer that looked like a photocopy machine with video screens. She told Felice that often enough people had to be called back for the old ink-based fingerprints, because fingerprints wear away, and the electronic ridges of light and shadow that the digitizer creates don't always show enough detail.

"Your fingerprints wear away?" This was news to Felice.

"Some folks sandpaper 'em, but other things will do it. Age, work."

"I was a printer once—used kerosene to wash the presses and was too young to know better and wear rubber gloves."

"That could do it. And you're old enough."

Felice didn't expect that any of the things her fingerprints might turn up would matter to the volunteer coordinator, who didn't miss a beat when Felice asked if out lesbians were welcome as tutors. Still, she was curious. What did the machine read in her hand? Perhaps now would be a good time to invoke the Freedom of Information act and take a look at her file.

How many files can they keep? Recently, the FBI had called up the contact woman for Women in Black, which held a vigil once a month in San Francisco to protest the treatment of Palestinians by Israel, to show support for a Palestinian state, and demand the evacuation of Israeli settlements. The contact woman had refused to speak to the FBI. On the alternate radio station, KPFA, the contact woman said if the FBI thought a group of mostly lesbian, mostly Jewish, mostly middle-aged women peace activists were the confidants of fundamentalist Islamic men, they had a more tenuous grasp on contemporary politics than any of us would have believed. Felice had started going to Women in Black vigils regularly back in the spring, moved to action by eye-witness e-mails from the Middle East.

About a month ago, she had lunch with a cousin who lived in Israel whom she hadn't seen in more than thirty years. The cousin was a thoughtful woman, who said, "When this started, we should have dropped flowers and candy through all the occupied territories, along with the message, 'Let's talk.' It would have done two things—shown our strength, and that we had an openness, a sense of humor. But then," she said, somewhat apologetically, "I'm a child of the '60s." Her husband had a sour look, as if he wanted to say, "What can you expect from a woman? They don't understand war." But at least he knew he was outnumbered at the table.

Felice had been twenty minutes early for her first afternoon as a tutor, so she passed the school and kept driving. International Boulevard runs the length of Oakland, and once it leaves downtown and heads south, is the kind of wasteland strip cities big enough to have slums disown. Fast food joints and greasy spoons—Chinese, Vietnamese, Mexican, Soul food—cozy up to auto body shops, meat markets, dollar clothing stores, ministries, boarded-up buildings, with the occasional elementary school and funeral parlor.

What makes a section of town look poor? This was not an idle question for Felice. Trash, old paint, bars, no trees. When International crossed into San Leandro, it became a pleasant boulevard almost immediately, complete with sidewalk flower boxes, interesting shops and restaurants with big plate windows, whether or not you'd want to eat in them. Entrepreneurs on the Oakland side, on too much of a shoe string budget, hand-lettered their own signs: *Pierda Pesos Aqui!* Qwik Loan Store. Her lover said that when the change is so dramatic from one town to the next, it must have something to do with public policy. The city of Oakland wanted this part to be ugly, depressing. She drove past a beautiful unreinforced masonry building from another time—a gingerbread concoction of orange and red brick—with an "office space available" sign and broken windows, then turned around. She made a right onto 69th Street after consulting the map the organization gave her in the volunteers' handbook.

Volunteers were supposed to park on the side street beside the playground. The playground was a wide sheet of fenced-in asphalt with dumpsters along the side and a small open door in the ten-foot high fencing by the cafeteria, where the girls' program was supposed to be. Felice, still early, kept the alternate news radio station on and read the "Letters to the Editor" in the San Francisco gay paper, in which suddenly patriotic men complained about the blood banks' refusal to take gay guys' blood, and women espousing left-wing theories reiterated the reasons why people in other parts of the world might hate us.

She had been told to meet the site coordinator between 3:00 and 3:15 inside the gate, and at 3:01, Felice locked the car and walked over. No one was around. She saw the small sign for the girls' program above a door, but the door was locked. She walked around the side of the building and a man in a truck asked her what she was doing. "I'm a literacy volunteer. No school today?"

"Nope, no school for the children," he said.

When Felice was young, all the schools back East closed for Columbus Day, which in Berkeley was now called Indigenous Peoples' Day. Oakland was always unpredictable. When Felice had called to find out about closures, the volunteer coordinator told her to look at the school schedule in the appendix of the volunteers' handbook, which absolutely did not list October 8th, the closest Monday to October 12th, as a holiday. "I didn't think we observed that here," the coordinator said.

Clearly she was wrong. Felice had enjoyed Columbus Day as a child because it was so close to her birthday, and no one had told her yet about the attempted genocide of Native Americans. Once her father had taken her into New York on Columbus Day weekend to see the rodeo, which she thought silly—even at eight-years-old, Roy Rogers' horse pawing the dust as if to count struck her as among the more pathetic forms of entertainment—and it was smelly too. What she liked was the Planetarium—leaning back in the big plush seats to learn about the mysteries of ancient myths configured in the constellations made her imagination tingle.

The girls in the literacy program, she was fairly sure, did not get taken into San Francisco to go to museums in Golden Gate Park, although possibly they were taken to local fairs—Juneteenth, Dia de Los Muertos, Chinese New Year celebrations, which all happened on International Boulevard. The handbook had statistics about the girls' parents—fifty-eight percent never got out of high school, only three percent had finished college. She felt a voyeuristic unease about knowing this. She was going to go into a group of six and seven year old girls knowing they were poor and their parents were uneducated in the ways that institutional cultures valued. Sometimes she felt joyful about the prospect, but today she felt like the representative of the men bombing Afghanistan—*the missionary of reading! democracy is hope! your future is what you want it to be!*

She got back in her car and waited, in case the man in the truck was wrong somehow, in case the after school program met anyway. A few cars pulled up, a group of older students—junior high, probably—walked through the buildings farther away, across the asphalt, toward the small gate. Apparently only the elementary school children got the holiday. Two or three parents in cars waited. Felice got out again, to check. She looked at the side of the cafeteria where the girls' program was held. The ugly beige paint was faded, and various things had been thrown against the side—splotches that did not invite close inspection. What makes this school worse than others? Why isn't it painted, kept clean? Does the city really parcel out resources to public schools based on the tax rate of the districts?

She remembered that when she taught college English, one of her sentence combining exercises was based on a news article about Vermont, which had decided to allocate the same amount of funds to all public schools, regardless of location. A few outraged Vermonters called it socialism; the article surprised her because it was the first time she really understood that "public" education was an elaborate hoax, despite personally knowing Oakland elementary school teachers who didn't have enough paper for their classrooms. Why wouldn't every adult automatically agree that all school children should have the same resources? The Junior League members and the woman who had baited her about feminism at the orientation meeting had all chosen to volunteer at the whiter San Leandro school, but the African American and Latina volunteers had chosen this one. This was the closest school to where Felice had lived in Oakland for eighteen years now. Why shouldn't she come here?

Felice loved language. Her father had read her Kipling and Vachel Lindsay as a child, for the heavy rhyme patterns and the "Boots, Boots, Boots/ Marching up and down again/ And there's no discharge in the war," which always sent her brother and her into giggles. Her mother sat on the side of her bed and read her nursery rhymes. *Mother Goose comes down the hill, to see if she can take your ills, puts them in a paper sack, now you know they won't come back.*

She gave up on the site coordinator showing up. What should she do? An unexpected two hour break—she decided to explore the neighborhood a little in her car. She drove past a gated housing project that had the barren concrete aspect of a prison, toward the BART station, going left and right down random streets, trying not to look like a lost tourist. She noticed that several side streets had small houses jammed up against each other—dilapidated row houses. It's the jamming together, the absence of trees, the old cars leaking oil in the streets, trash cans a dog knocks over and no one picks up, the liquor store on the corner with bars in the windows that make a place look hard to grow up in.

A woman walked unsteadily from the liquor store into the center of the street and motioned to Felice.

Felice slowed in the intersection and looked in the woman's face, which seemed as boarded up as a burned building, no light coming from within. The woman held out her hand, in which a glob of some drug poked out from a paper sheath.

"Looking for something?" the woman asked.

"No, I don't want to buy anything," Felice said, too loudly. She drove quickly back to the main street that led up the hill.

The value of a book, they used to say, was that it opened up worlds to you. You could travel anywhere, be anyone.

Next week she'd come back and try again.

PRESSURE

The herbalist tells Felice she has to think of something that gives her peace when she gets her blood pressure taken. "Think of some beautiful place, and breathe in. Imagine you are walking there, at ease. Have you got it?"

"Yes," she says, yet she lies. She is imagining a snow-covered field, a scrunch of boot on a thin, unbroken covering of ice. But the field turns into a cemetery, the old Conway cemetery where she had wanted to be buried, where her first dog, running with a dog pack, tore apart a squirrel, in a little hollow below the cemetery hill. Is that going to bring her blood pressure down?

"Hmm," the herbalist says. "Two points. Practice this at home. I've seen people bring down their blood pressure quite a bit by visualization."

She has a little automatic blood pressure kit—half automatic. She pumps up the air, and the machine gives a reading. She bought the kit that does the calculation because she hadn't thought she'd be good at hearing the blood in her veins, whatever whoop and knock doctors listen to, measuring. Veins have always frightened her—not blood, blood she's fine with, more or less. She can gut a fish and take a razor to a splinter that's grown into an infected mound. When she turns her head away from phlebotomists in the blood lab, it's not because she doesn't like to see her own juice filling up the little color coded vials—it's the needle going into the vein. When she was little—five or six—she would lie in bed frightened that such delicate things ran over the sturdy bones, a soft lace under the skin. What keeps them from collapsing? She must have heard that veins can collapse, or rupture, or explode. One of her aunts must have been going into gory detail about a medical tragedy. She was a child listening to her heart, to the sounds of her body. If she moved suddenly, would her veins fall in? Would they turn soft as noodles, shutting the blood away from the hungry cells, waiting for nourishment?

In her thirties, she had a dream that she was crawling through tunnels under the sea, old tunnels, branching in many directions. Some of the branches were closed, and she could barely make out writing on the ground, embedded into crumbling tile. "What is still strong will hold." When she woke, she knew that she had been looking into her own arteries—walking around inside herself, checking out the structure, which was adequate now but decaying.

Still, when her blood pressure started going up about ten years later, she was surprised. After all, they were supposed to be Amazons, impervious to the regular laws of physics. And since she had been one of those lesbians who never thought she'd live past twenty-seven—certain to be felled by suicidal despair or some dramatic consequence of the risks she took—she was unprepared for ordinary mortality catching up. She had muscular problems, a torn kneepad and bad feet, but those were structural in a different way, and could be ameliorated, if not cured, through devices, moderate exercise, relatively innocuous drugs.

Now the herbalist tells her to visualize. As she squeezes the little rubber bulb on her home device, she closes her eyes. A place of peace. The cemetery isn't it. She looks out the window at the bottlebrush, and a large yellow butterfly traces the fence line, then disappears. She sighs. California is sweet and dry, the hills turning yellow brown, a large date palm visible a block away. But is California peaceful? Can you lower your blood pressure by saying: *this is my home and I am happy here?* Apparently not.

But for almost a year, the herbs work anyway. Her blood pressure stays mostly under 85—the diastolic, the one the doctors say counts the most—even when she travels, or eats salty food, which she still likes. She keeps working on what she visualizes while taking her blood pressure, although her theory is that you should visualize a car crash, so you'll know the worst. You want to get an accurate reading, don't you? Why not strive for the reading you'd have if you were under stress, so you'll know precisely how much you can take? If being rear-ended is going to give you a heart attack, wouldn't you want to know? Then again, anticipating disaster and being in one are very different.

The real disasters are these ordinary things that push us toward change we would not choose. What happens when your blood pressure gets too high? Stroke, they say—because the walls of the veins and arteries, covered now with an accumulation of some kind of internal dung, tough yellow cholesterol deposits like bat guano, stretch with stress and can't relax, can't go back to their normal resting selves. Eventually they get worn out and you spring a leak. The leak is not good for you, really not good if it happens in your brain or your heart, but not good anywhere.

She has trouble breathing when she tries to think about this, and realizes how spotty her knowledge is, how full of fragments from the Sunday paper magazine supplements. What is a stroke? She doesn't want to know. And now she's convinced she's going to die of one. Stroke or heart attack. Her grandmother had a bad heart, and her mother has some kind of heart problem—her mother gets an aura and passes out once in awhile, though medication and moving to a retirement community seem to have that under control—but then they smoked. A lot. She hasn't smoked since shortly after college, and she never smoked more than a pack on a rare, speed-freak day.

But she read somewhere that amphetamine makes the walls of the veins that go through your brain weak. Only there? A localized effect? Some softness waiting to trip you up, to make you pay for what you did when you were seventeen and could not imagine being fifty? All that changes from twenty-five to fifty is the body, the experience that accumulates in the body. Is memory a form of cholesterol? If you lower your cholesterol will you forget the taste of cheese—reblochon, say, that came on a cheese plate one night in the south of France? Will you forget France, and Fanny laughing as the map blows out the window on your way to the Feminist Book Fair? Does cultivating an austerity of one sense bode ill for the others?

She's grateful to the herbalist, a big dyke, not unlike herself. Many years ago, in her Saturn cycle (oh you know, it's that terrible time you go through at the end of your twenties, when the planets more or less realign themselves to the position they were in when you were born and for reasons that make no sense to her, that alignment appears to tear your life apart), she left the town she was living in, alone in a van that had been remade into a shop teacher's idea of a recreational vehicle. She had been reading herbals, all about the properties of flowers and leaves, branches and stems, what they can do boiled up into teas, or rolled into poultices. She believes in the natural world—why not? It always makes more sense than the unnatural world, a world of cars and cell phones, even if the unnatural world is more fun.

In her homemade RV, she had twenty or thirty jars of herbs, which she experimented with, making herself concoctions to ease her anxiety (a woman staying alone in campgrounds or behind lesbians' houses, traveling in the South), and her conscience—for not staying where she had been and finding a way to work things out. Her relationship had clearly been a lost cause, but she should have kept wrestling with the Women's Center, stayed in the storm of lesbian politics. Skullcap didn't work well on her—it constricted something in her scalp, which pounded back against the constriction. But otherwise, she recognized that herbs had direct effects and were useful. Long after her attention was diverted to other things, she believed in the restorative properties of plants.

Homeopathy, that's a different matter. Like astrology, she understands why other people believe in it. When sick with a cold, she has Fanny consult a pendulum to find out what remedy she should take. Her lover says that the beauty of homeopathy is that you don't have to believe in it for it to work. But Felice never thinks it really works for her anyway, belief or no belief. Something about a tiny drop—a microscopic speck—of the thing that's wrong with you being the cure—tried her patience. And she couldn't feel it.

Too pragmatic, she supposes: only believe in what you can see or what has a reasonable explanation. Was that true of her? She knows that spirits exist, though she can't see them. She knows that time is full of tricks, a contortionist, insinuating itself into distance, which we measure in hours. This year she goes on a book tour of Germany and England, fourteen readings in fifteen nights, every day a different train, eating whatever is put before them in smoky restaurants and bars, the intensity of meeting new dykes, saying goodbye, meeting new dykes. When she gets home, her blood pressure and cholesterol are creeping past borderline, too high. Maybe it has nothing to do with what you eat, but what you sense: the ghosts of Europe crowding against the permeable membrane of the present. *Can the body really be affected by what you see when you close your eyes?*

Everyone says so now. Cancer and AIDS researchers have careful theories about laughter and meditational breathing. It's important not to blame individuals for the ills we suffer—no one was ever cured by being shamed for having unprotected sex or eating fried chicken. But surely some part of the body's response is within our control? More radical health workers say that these diseases are environmental: sludge in the air, hormones in the meat, pesticides on the vegetables, in the water supply, wind-borne radiation leaks. Encouraging people to think that by completely controlling their diets, getting rid of everything in their houses that isn't natural fiber, spending hours each day practicing breathing is to remove those people from collective action, from making common cause with each other.

Easy to say when it's not you. Your blood pressure goes up—you want to make it go back down. What would you do to make that happen? What would you pay? She tries to do what the herbalist says: cut out salts and all oils except olive, no animal fats, no fried food, no white sugar, honey's okay. This is extremely difficult even though she's been working towards it for a long time. It's not the food: spicy hummus and free-range turkey on organic bread, salmon broiled in hot sauce, olive oil and gin; sulfite-free red wine, blueberries in soy milk, carrot juice, trail mix, vegetarian "beef" jerky. It's good to live in California, the land of fresh fruit. A little salt, a little cheese stay in her diet, but she cuts way back on them. What she hates is how this change reminds her of the old female prison of dieting. She tries to eat whenever she's hungry, as much as she wants. *How long does it take to come to terms with what we eat?* She asked this question twenty years ago. Now she knows eating requires more compassion for yourself than sex. At least in sex, if you're lucky (and she is, finally), someone else is there. But sex is a happy circumstance even if indulged in once a month; eating "right" takes a lot of time. Maybe, she hopes, it will quickly become eating again and she can get back to work—once she's found the sweet rolls made with honey and organic nuts and gets used to drinking the clover, nettle and oat straw tea the herbalist prescribes.

The herbalist lives in a modest house on a modest street with a nice garden. One of her clients built her a wall cabinet for the bottles of herbal infusions—it has a hundred or more pigeonholes, designed for the bottle size. You go around the back, through the garden, to a small free-standing room where the bottles and books are. It's quiet back there. While the herbalist feels your pulses, you can look out the window at squirrels eating peanuts from a tree feeder. The herbalist asks you questions about your sleep habits, your bowels, the way you feel about others, the way you feel when you're alone. After making copious notes, she takes out five, six, seven, eight bottles and puts together a mixture. Sometimes she has you lick a small dose of something, so she can watch how it affects you. "Did you feel how your chest softened?" "Yes," you say, though what does that mean, a softening chest? She charges $54 most of the time, which includes the remedy, as long as you bring back the empty bottle. This takes about an hour, and you have to take the potion three times a day.

Certainly all this should leave enough time over for collective action. But when something is wrong in your body, you get stuck there. She feels stuck. Listening to the closed up sound of liquid pushing through the veins. She tries to visualize. Squish, squish, squish, the cuff tightens. She exhales, which sounds more like a sigh. What does she see behind her eyes?

Often she sees Fanny's awe, that first afternoon in the Rockies in their first week as lovers. Fanny had never seen the Rockies before, never driven cross country. Fanny lived in the East, while Felice lived in California, but Fanny was changing her life that year before turning fifty, moving across country without a job or a place to live, only a direction, a necessity. How they met was a long story, but they'd known of each other for eight or nine years, as friends of friends.

She has that image of Fanny at a waterfall in the Rockies, raising her arms up. In that gesture, Fanny released the East Coast, its constraints, her miserable childhood, her unhappy marriage, her heterosexual celibacy, the difficulty of coming out and entering dyke community at age forty. Fanny raised her hands over her head and the West roared over them, a new life.

This image makes her smile, the kind of smile in which your upper lip curls, genuine physical pleasure, remembered. But then remembering waterfalls leads to other thoughts—a day at Burney Falls up by Lassen, rowing on the lake, seeing her first bald eagle. Then thinking of eagles reminds her of how pesticides have entered the food chain, making eggshells unnaturally thin, imperiling the lives of the raptors. Certainly this cannot be good for your blood pressure. And the fountain in the corner of the dining room is merging with the memory of waterfalls, making her have to pee.

She tries again. She presses down on her eyelids, now looking for the perfect black. When she tried doing exercises for her eyes, that's what the book said: "Imagine the darkest black you can." That was when she was a printer, and the darkest black she knew shined, the black of ink in the ink tray of a printing press. Viscous, darker than city nights, compelling, the ink from which all letters materialize, this brings her relief for a moment.

The little blood pressure machine beeps and she stops pumping. She keeps her eyes closed, listening to it count down. Deet deet deet deet—how far down will it go? Black, look into the ink tray. It stops at 142 over 92. Not good. Still not good. The herbalist has told her a story of a man who brought his blood pressure down ten points right in front of her. Is she not capable of the same spiritual focus as some guy? Can she not keep her attention on anything peaceful, something that won't transform into complication? The ocean at sunset throws up syringes, dead fish.

The dog whose color matched the redwoods died—some kind of stroke, explosion or implosion in her brain. The hummingbird, the butterfly, the red bottlebrush bush, the evening light, the first lesbian bar she went to in Greenwich Village, her lover laughing in delight, coming towards her—if she can grin, why can't she relax?

The herbalist listens patiently. Wants to know if she has a little melancholy. *Yes, in a drawer downstairs, I take it out and polish it on the full moon.* "Yes, a little."

"All right," the herbalist pulls out a big book, consults the index. "Here it is. Do you lie awake thinking about your death?"

"Well, yes, I guess. Especially now that I can't bring my blood pressure down."

The herbalist shows her the illustration. "You know there's a cactus that only blooms once a year, at night. Night-blooming Cereus."

"Yes, I remember that. Shani Mootoo wrote a book with that name—a very good dyke novel—about imperialism and being lesbians."

The herbalist looks up. "What's it called?"

"*Cereus Blooms At Night.* You should look for it—with a C, right?"

"Right." The herbalist looks back at the book. "This is intense. Usually they list the medicinal properties and then give the contraindications. But for this one, they put the toxic effects up front, what happens with an overdose."

"Oh. What's a toxic effect look like?"

"Usually I don't tell my clients—I use a lot of things that could be a poison in the wrong dose. And I'm giving you a very small amount of this. Basically, everything that it's supposed to cure gets worse. Palpitations, anxiety, fear of death. Taste it."

She licks the drops in her hand. They're sweet, and carry the taste of the brandy which is their base. Usually the remedies are bitter or taste like wood pulp, the ash of rotten flowers that have been gathered after a forest fire.

"What do you feel?"

She sighs. How can she know if she feels different than a second ago? All she knows is she wants to feel different, and hopes she isn't being poisoned. This is when the herbalist says her chest has softened. She relaxes, dropping her shoulders a little.

"Queen of the Night. If I was sick," the herbalist says, "I'd want to take something called Queen of the Night."

This surprises her. She imagines that the herbalist is always doing little experimentations on herself. And she thinks that all women are in some state of sickness, of needing to be better, stronger, clearer, cleaner, healthier than they are—that the division between herself and the herbalist is one of degrees, not states of being. She doesn't think of herself as sick—but as a dyke with a bum knee and trouble concentrating.

"Trouble concentrating? You mean trouble with motivation?"

"Yes, trouble having motivation," she says, although it's really a problem with ambition. She can't believe in the reason why anyone does anything—we have to do things, and there's pleasure in doing, in being alive. But what we do—what difference does it make? Or is that only a way to excuse herself for not going down to the garment workers office and seeing what she can do about sweatshops in her own city, from volunteering to do writing workshops for adolescent girls at the local queer center? Of course she is having trouble with motivation; she can't even visualize her damn blood pressure down.

The herbalist takes out a tray of flower remedies, also made from cactuses, and puts a few drop into the potion, which, besides

Queen of the Night, has at least six other ingredients, including Hawthorn. The drops are from the Saguaro cactus—here Felice can see Arizona at night from the car window quite clearly. Taking in the spirit of the big desert cactus towers, their shapes almost human, stroking the wide evening, sounds like a good idea. Her last long-time lover's mother, who lived in Tucson, showed them how to identify wildflowers in the desert. She can visualize that. But that mother is dead now, and she's never finished the story she meant to write about her.

"This will give you a psychic kick in the pants."

"That's what I need," she says, "a psychic kick in the pants."

She takes the remedy that night, cautiously, checking for signs of overdose, thinking that she should worry about her death, but overcome quickly by sleep. In the morning she takes it again. Mid-afternoon when she checks her blood pressure, it's 140 over 83. She would like to leave it there: Queen of the Night is the cure. But weeks go by. Some mornings her head feels like someone is blowing up a balloon under her skin—not tightening, exactly, just the body straining against itself unpleasantly. On these days her blood pressure nudges up—148 over 87, 89.

Maybe it's entering peri-menopause. She hasn't bled for two months, not since she stayed in the women's guesthouse in East Berlin. Unreleased eggs are rotting in her ovaries, turning to mush. She has sworn to herself that she's going to get through "the change" without hormone replacement, which has always seemed counterintuitive to her—the body changes, you need not to postpone that, but to live through it, note it, get to the other side. For thousands of years, women have gone into menopause without medical intervention. For thousands of years, women have died young.

Do you think about your death? Once a friend of hers had a lover who claimed to have never considered suicide. "She's not

deep enough for you, then," she told the friend. Shortly after-
wards, they broke up. Who doesn't think about their death?
Lying in bed at night with the cars prowling on the ridge, her
lover snores lightly, skooched down thoughtfully so that the
snores will bounce off her elbow, not her face. She believes Fanny
will outlive her, that one day she will be gone. Everything she
thought or tried—every mistake, every revelation, hope, hunger,
procrastination—erased. The planet will change, scab up over its
human wounds, and then the universe will scab over the hole left
when this solar system is gone. No wonder people want to believe
in god, another realm where our importance does not diminish,
where thought is collected, cherished, enshrined.

She takes a breath: *I will not give in to death. Tonight I will
imagine my veins relaxed and strong, uncluttered with debris. I will
not be afraid.* She closes her eyes and visualizes the queen of the
night, opening in a dark wind.

SALT OF THE EARTH

I had a dream: I spilled a sack of salt in the road. "No matter," my friends said, "we don't need salt."

But I remembered my grandmother sending me little burlap bags of salt from Florida, and I said: *That's the trouble with us. Salt is an electrolyte, we need it to conduct electricity, the good feelings between us. No wonder we don't have the connections we need. We don't have enough salt.*

In my dream, I decided to call up every lesbian I could and tell them: *You are the salt of the Earth.*

But when I woke I thought, *Damn, how am I going to do this, where am I going to find the time and the self-assurance to say, over and over again: "You don't know me, but my dreams have given me the mission to spread my message: you are the salt of the Earth." It's an old message, but worth repeating.*

I mean, how many times could I bear to have lesbians hang up on me?

Then I remembered this book. What better place to start?

You are the salt of the Earth. Pass it on.

ABOUT THE AUTHOR

Elana Dykewomon has been a cultural worker and activist since the 1970s. Her books include *Riverfinger Women, Nothing Will Be As Sweet As The Taste*–Selected Poems, and the Jewish lesbian historical novel *Beyond the Pale*, which received the Lambda and Ferro-Grumley (Gay & Lesbian Publishers Triangle Association) awards for lesbian fiction in 1998. Recent work has appeared in *The Journal of Lesbian Studies, Love Shook My Heart II* and *This Bridge Called Home*. She brought the international lesbian feminist journal of arts and politics, *Sinister Wisdom*, to the San Francisco Bay Area in 1987, serving as an editor for nine years, and now lives in Oakland with her lover among friends, writing, teaching and trying to stir up trouble whenever she can.

Spinsters Ink Books

Spinsters Ink Books is one of the oldest feminist publishing houses in the world. It was founded in upstate New York in 1978, and is now located in Denver, Colorado.

The noun "spinster"means a woman who spins. The definition of the verb "spin" is to whirl and twirl, to revert, to spin on one's heels, to turn everything upside down. Spinsters Ink books do just that—take women's "yarns" (stories, tales) and enable readers to see the world through the other end of the telescope. Spinsters Ink authors move readers off their comfort zones just a bit, pushing the camel through the eye of the needle. These are thinking books for thinking readers.

Spinsters Ink fiction and non-fiction titles deal with significant issues in women's lives from a feminist perspective. They not only name these crucial issues but—more importantly—encourage change and growth. We are committed to publishing works by women writing from the periphery: fat women, Jewish women, lesbians, old women, immigrant women, poor women, rural women, women examining classism, women of color, women with disabilities, women involved in social justice issues, women who are writing books that help make the best in our lives more possible.

To Order Books
Spinsters Ink titles are available at your local booksellers or through Spinsters Ink Books. Call 1-800-301-6860 to place an order. A free catalog is available upon request or visit www.spinsters-ink.com. You may order directly online, or mail your order to: Spinsters Ink Books, P.O. Box 22005, Denver CO 80222. Please include $3.00 shipping and handling for the first title ordered, 50¢ for every title thereafter. All major credit cards accepted.

Other Titles Available from Spinsters Ink Books